Edgar
A Story About Love. And Zombies. And Pizza.
By Jason Appling

Dedicated to anyone who has been constantly harping on me to write a book. You said you would buy it. Hopefully, you haven't changed your mind.

Because that's really not cool at all.

1.

THEY SAY the journey of 1,000 miles begins with a single step. God knows I have taken more than my share of that equation. The air around me is brisk this morning. The leaves crumble into soft dust beneath my feet. If I had any painting skills at all, I would be able to make Bob Ross himself weep at how happy the trees look today against the serenity of the purples and pinks of the morning sky.

It would be idyllic for anyone to get married on a day like this. I can completely picture the groom standing at the altar and the bride sauntering down the aisle. Everyone's head is turned towards her with joyous expressions on their faces, the little flower girl dumping the mass of rose petals all in one clump and everyone laughing about it. The ring bearer boy too busy playing with a fidget spinner to notice his cue to walk down with the pillow. More laughter. The exchange of vows, the walk out as husband and wife, the reception where the uncle gets so hammered that he starts telling stories to embarrass the groom, and someone shoving coffee in his face before he gets totally creepy and hits on the bridesmaids who just turned eighteen and just want to take selfies so that they can get back to their jobs at Dairy De-lite to serve the locals their milkshakes and burgers.

Yep. It would be idyllic, indeed.

But that's not possible.

Despite the image I just described to you, it's not possible because there aren't people anymore. Nothing really remains. The weather and nature are still here, yet humanity is nonexistent as far as I can tell. The buildings remain, and I can still recognize what most of them used to be, but they're all desolate and ransacked. I'm unsure as to what happened, or how it all went down, but I am certain of two things:
1. My name is Edgar.
2. I'm a zombie.

Now, I have a good idea of what's going through your head. It probably sounds a little like this:

"OH, GREAT. ANOTHER BOOK ABOUT ZOMBIES. PRETTY SURE THIS IS GOING TO BE ALL ABOUT HIM EATING BRAINS. I ALREADY KNOW WHAT HAPPENS ON EVERY ZOMBIE SHOW EVER MADE AND I OWN *ZOMBIE CHEERLEADERS FROM PLANET CORNBALL* ON VHS, DVD, AND THE COLLECTOR'S EDITION ON BLU-RAY. I READ HOW TO SURVIVE THE APOCALYPSE, AND I HAVE SUBSCRIBED TO NUMEROUS YOUTUBE CHANNELS TO SURVIVE IT."

Am I right?

Based upon all that experience, you would last exactly less than two seconds out here. I'm not saying I'm a tough guy zombie by any stretch of the imagination, in fact when I was human, I was your standard nerd. Conventions about gaming, lots of sack lunches, and pizza rolls and Mountain Dew for days, son. No. Women. Anywhere.

But the fact is, this place kind of sucks. Sure there are other zombies, but there's not really any way we can talk to each other. I only know my thoughts. It's actually really hard to know what another zombie is thinking. It's not like our facial expressions change all that much. I mean, yeah, a jaw might fall off of Peter and you'd think: "damn. Did Peter do something with his hair this morning? He's always been on the cutting edge of post-apocalyptic fashion, but this is a whole other level."

And then you realize. Nope. Just his jaw has fallen off.

We've gotten a really bad reputation with Hollywood slandering our names, but the truth is that we're not that much different from the ones who have survived the outbreak. We want a place to call our own, maybe to start a community, and if we're really dreaming big, perhaps a Target to do our shopping in.

The problem is that our communication isn't that great. Hollywood did manage to get that right about us, but they failed to mention the complexities that exist in the brains of the undead. Like me, for example. I hate, HATE the word "undead". It's totally insensitive. Aren't any of the ones who haven't turned ALSO "undead"? I mean, they haven't died, right? But, no. Zombies don't get those types of luxuries. And ENOUGH WITH THE WHOLE BRAIN EATING THING. WE DON'T WANT TO EAT ANYONE'S BRAINS AT ALL.

Yes, you get hungry. Are *you* hungry reading this right now? Oh, look! I bet you're human and all. With your 98 degree flesh and wifi connections in all your cafes. Just reading this book like: "Dang, Edgar. Not only do you have a horrifically craptastic name, but you have to eat people's brains to live? That's horrible! I could never be a zombie!"

Well, yeah. You couldn't survive the apocalypse, and you couldn't be a zombie. So now that we have narrowed those two things down, what is it that you *can* do? The only thing I can do is walk and grunt at other zombies. Sometimes, if I'm really feeling like I have my sassypants on, and I see a female zombie that I'm attracted to, I'll grunt for longer than I normally would. Like it was in life before, however, she usually just creeps past me like I don't even exist. People often wonder why zombies walk around aimlessly so much. It's usually just to find a place, but more often than not, we're looking for food. Calm down, tough guy. We aren't looking for you specifically. We're just looking for food. As everything is pretty much abandoned, we have to keep walking. And you know what I would really kill for? What I crave more than anything in this entire destroyed earth?

Pizza.

Yeah. Bet you didn't see that one coming, did you?

Problem: there are no functioning pizza places at all anymore. If there was a working microwave, and a grocery store that wasn't shredded, I would even eat those 99 cent frozen pizzas. You know the ones I'm talking about. Don't act like you don't. The ones where you're at a party, and the most hammered guy is just sitting in a corner and chewing on that cardboard made to look like pizza? With the little cubes that are supposed to be pepperoni?

That's what I miss the most about the old world. If I could just find even one slice of pizza and have a little place of my own, and a gray-fleshed beauty of a woman to settle down with, that would be living the dream. Or "unliving" the dream. Stupid term. See what I mean with the whole "undead" thing?

But I'm going to keep walking until I find it. I don't care if I have to walk to the ends of this earth. I don't care if both of my legs fall off. I will have that pizza before it's all said and done.

My name is Edgar.

And this is my story.

No—wait. Let's call it a quest. Yes. Edgar's Quest For Pizza.

Actually, scrap that. We'll just go with this is my story.

2.

LIKE I mentioned before, getting pizza in this place is nothing short of miraculous. I would probably have better luck winning the lottery or predicting the when the next five blades of grass are going to grow, and where they will spring up. It just hurts me knowing that I will more than likely never be reunited with my one true love. No time to think about such things however. It's time to get up and get going with my day.

My daily routine is pretty basic. I get up, stretch out for a little bit, and begin my walk into town. It takes me a little longer than it normally would, but there again, I don't want to waste energy unnecessarily. I also tend to get lost on the way. No GPS and all. I usually encounter other zombies on the way, and we do the basic greeting. If you don't know what that looks like, it's a little like when two drunk people see each other in a bar and sort of recognize each other. We stand still, sway in the breeze, grunt at each other for a few seconds and then stagger on. I try not to look anyone in the eyes. I made that mistake early on when I saw a female zombie from behind.

She was staggering towards her destination, and her hair was chunky and caked with dirt. Her flesh seemed to be illuminated by the sun, so I figured I would get over to her and lay on by most smooth grunt to inform the fair maiden that I was interested,. It took me a while to get to her, but she ran into a tree and couldn't figure out the whole how to get around the obstacle thing. Like, she just kept running into the tree. Over. And over. And over.

I get along beside her. Oh, man. This is going to be it.

I grunt. Softly. Longingly.

Mmmrpummph. Mrrrrummmmphpumphpuhmph.

She turns.

Let's totally ignore the fact that SHE HAS A BEARD, and focus rather on her eyes.

Eye.

The other one was this cavernous void that had, from what I could tell, every last maggot on the planet stacked inside.

DEAR GOD WHY. NOT ONLY DID I THINK THIS WAS A GIRL, BUT I MAY HAVE FOUND THE ZOMBIE VERSION OF EVERY ALLMAN BROTHERS FAN SINCE CREATION STARTED.. PLUS MAGGOTS. TRULY, I HAVE HIT THE JACKPOT.

Bottom line: if you and I ever meet on the street, and I don't look you in the eyes, it's not because I'm being rude, it's just that I have nightmares now from seeing the face that should be on the cover of every death metal album for the next thirty years.

Anyway, like I said, getting into town can be a bit of a challenge. I never really know where I'm going, and I follow people who I am pretty sure have less of a clue than I do. There are abandoned cars all along the side of the road, and all throughout what used to be the highways. If you don't know how difficult it is to get to places when roads aren't really an option, feel free to go sauntering about through the woods in order to get to a local establishment without ever setting foot on a road. Best of luck with that, Davey Crockett. Let me know how that works out for you.

Eventually, we end up in town. Town is always a mixed bag for me. Like I said, I can remember how most things were before I turned, but everything is different now. The windows have been boarded up, there is always some halfie in the street (a halfie is a zombie who has been ripped in half. It's pretty cool looking when it's the top half, but when it's the lower torso, it just looks silly. Just legs flapping about in the breeze), and I can at least go inside the old coffee shop and pretend like I'm standing in line for my very important coffee of the day.

But the pizza calls to me. It's the thing that drives me the most. I try to go into as many places as humanly—zombiely—possible. Just for a taste of civilization. A meaning. A purpose.

I go into a store, and Greg is in there. I don't know if that's actually his name, but he just kind of looks like a Greg. In fact, I don't know anyone's name at all. I just kind of make up their names based upon what they look like and then create the back story from their different habits. Know what I mean?

And then I heard it.

Greg was standing next to me and chewing on some old drywall (that Greg. Always doing crazy things), and it was loud. Clear. Not in grunts.

Voices. Human voices.

Even Greg stopped chewing on the drywall and a piece fell from his teeth.

I look outside. There is a halfie dangling from a children's carousel outside of the We-Saves-A-Lot. She is groaning and pointing in the direction of where I bought my first comic book.

I look.

There are five of them. Their flesh isn't gray. They even appear to be sweating profusely, which is strange given the fall like weather. They're heavily armed, and pointing guns in all directions as they advance towards the halfie. One pulls out a knife, and slams it into the halfie's temple. The halfie is no longer doing anything. I try to put my hand over my mouth to avoid from making noise, but my coordination isn't what it used to be anymore, so I end up slapping myself in the face. This noise alerts Greg, and, genius that he is, takes it as a sign to attempt to go and run towards the group. Greg makes it maybe about six steps, and he is the equivalent of Swiss cheese. Zombie style.

I panic. I turn to run as fast as I can out of the store, as they must have a back door somewhere. The voices are getting louder, and they are yelling something about "another one in there". Bullets zip past my head, and I finally find the back door. It's locked. Of course it's locked. I guess people must have figured that zombies don't do well with locked doors, and I am no exception. I mean, it's not like being a zombie gives you super lock picking skills or anything, but in this situation, my joy would be unbridled if it did.

One of the positive things about the post-apocalypse is that there's all types of junk just lying around. I mean, had I taken some of those technical classes in high school, I would have been able to build my own place by now and not be in this predicament, but instead, I decided that I wanted to paint for a living. You know, like art and all that. The only way this could help me now is that if I could paint a tunnel so that I could escape like in the cartoons. Or maybe a big sign that reads: EDGAR IS A COOL GUY, AND JUST WANTS TO HAVE PIZZA. HE DOESN'T WANT TO EAT YOU. THE THOUGHT NEVER ONCE HAS CROSSED HIS MIND BECAUSE CANNIBALISM IS JUST KIND OF GROSS AND NOT A NICE THING TO DO TO PEOPLE IN GENERAL. Also, I have no paint nor time as these bloodthirsty savages get closer to my location. Think, Edgar. Think.

I find something to hit the door with as hard as I can. If it the door budged, it's because I fell down and my point of view was a bit shaky. Not exactly heroic. I try again. It seems the door has moved slightly. I repeat this process until there is enough room for me to squeeze through. I manage to become free, and I am sailing through the streets in an attempt to get away from whoever these people are. I smile as I run. Foolish humans! We are the future! This is our world! We shall rule it with an iron fist! We—

Crap. In my hasty escape attempt, I must have lost a hand squeezing through that door. I also notice a distinctive lean as I am standing.

Yep. A foot. I am down to one hand and one foot.

Fantastic.

Not the way I wanted to start my day.

3.

THAT WAS my first contact with humans since the outbreak. I hadn't seen any since I turned. I didn't have much use for them when we were all humans, and I certainly don't see me being a fan of theirs after all of that mess.

So many questions. Where did they get those guns from? Like did every redneck within a 50 mile radius just up and think: "hell yeah, buddy! Zawmbee uhpacuhlips! We's gonna go keel us sum zawmbies, buddy! Get tha budweiser from outback the truck and let's get ta basspro!"

What the hell, Jethro? You DO understand that we were just like you once, right? Okay, not exactly like you, but we were once all human. Greg. Greg was probably the manager of a local tire shop and might have had a cup by the register filled with those bank lollipops for the kids. He probably had a wife, and her name was more than likely Sarah. They probably even had Salisbury steak night every Thursday while they watched television. Sarah even might have had a dream to sell makeup stuff on the internet. And here you guys show up with an arsenal that would embarrass most small nations and turn my buddy Greg into a mass of crimson paste. Seriously, guys? You jest, right? What if Greg was running at you just because he was happy to see you? We haven't seen *actual* humans as long as I can recall, and you just do all that?

ALSO I AM MISSING A HAND AND A FOOT.

If I am to find pizza, the only way would probably be through those humans. I managed to scrape up a few crumbs of chips and something that might have been candy. Might have been sawdust. That's the other thing you humans don't understand about zombies. Your taste buds become slightly altered. And by slightly, I mean totally. Your body goes through changes.

Yes, I realize that last statement sounded like something my gym teacher was forced to read to us in sex education in middle school, but I don't know a better way to describe it. As far as I can remember about this new life of mine is that I was stepping outside of my house after an intense boss fight in a video game, I was tackled out of nowhere, and I've been a zombie ever since.

I would be more of a zombie if I had both hands and both feet. Still a little bitter about my new situation. Not going to lie.

I don't *want* to go back in town. Clearly if those humans are going to be there, they have made it highly apparent that we're not exactly going to be besties. I survey my new surroundings. It's getting dark, so I suppose I had better rest for the night. And by rest, I mean pace. For an incredibly long and awkward time.

As I thump along, a tear rolls softly down my rotting face. I thought I had missed pizza, but it turns out I miss my foot even more. And my hand. Because I can't wipe away the tear.

The dawn breaks, and it's time for me to face my fears. I must go back into town, pay my respects to the lump of Greg, and somehow muddle through this catastrophe. Needless to say, today's trip will take considerably longer with the noticeable absence of my foot. If you need a more visual idea, think about walking down a flight of steps and swearing there was one more step. You know that extra hard step you take and it feels like your innards have been shoved in your throat? Welcome to my new daily walk.

I get back into town, and there seems to be no more humans about. I hobble along the streets of the unfamiliar to see what has been left after these idiots have kept moving to whatever place they think is safe for them.

As a general rule, humans tend to ruin everything. I'm sure I was no different, but now that there are more zombies than humans, I notice it a lot more. With zombies, it's different. There's no great discussions on political ideologies, no HOAs to tend to, and for the most part, we keep to ourselves. I mean, it's not like humans would want to listen to our stories anyway, and even if they could, it would be nothing but an incessant string of grunts and groans. Not exactly what I would call stimulating conversation.

Other people (and I'm looking at you, Hollywood) tend to have this strange idea in their heads that because we can't articulate what's going on in our minds that we are somehow lacking them. Nothing could be farther from the truth. In fact, my mind is pretty much all I have left as my body is slowly deteriorating. It was bound to happen, after all. With social media being so prevalent in our lives before the outbreak, we were all adrift on this sea of mind numbing cat memes and the latest garbage on what celebrity went shopping that day. Useless clickbait garbage meant to fuel the fires of paranoia and outright hatred. It seems everyone just bought into it, and as a result, everything went into chaos when the outbreak happened. To that end, there's always been zombies. We were just too busy staring at our phones and our screens to notice.

Not bad philosophy for a guy who has festering sores up and down his arms, huh?

I guess that's why those humans acted the way they did when Greg decided to run to them with open arms. They probably just felt they were trying to protect whatever ideas of civilization they had left. I can't really understand why, though. We were more disconnected in society with one another than we are now. At least if I'm hanging out with a bunch of zombies and we're on our aimless walk for the day, there's no hidden agenda. No greed. Like I said earlier, just looking for a place to call home, and food on whatever table we can find.

. Charlie was most likely a busboy before the outbreak because he keeps trying to pick random items up off the ground like he's damned to eternally cleaning tables for the rest of his days. Steve? Steve's the quiet one. In his normal life, Steve was that friend you had that was insanely smooth with the ladies but wasn't a total jerk about it. You wanted to be Steve. All the guys did. I would bet if Greg was still with us, he and Steve would be friends. No doubt. They would probably even purchase matching airbrushed shirts to proclaim to the world that they are BFF, and after that they would get in Steve's van that has this kickass mural of *Star* Wars on the side of it and go on adventures.

And then there's Anna. Not only is her name the same spelled forwards and backwards, but time slowed as I stared at this luminous creature slowly staggering after a butterfly, but I felt my heart feel like it was about to come out of my chest whenever I laid eyes on her.

Seriously. My ribs and breastplate have been feeling a little mushy as of late due to decomposing. No telling when my heart will literally burst out of my chest. Probably not the best first impression. "Hey. I think you're really cool and pretty. Here's what my internal organs look like. Want to go and walk around aimlessly in the woods?" Not smooth, Edgar. Get it together, man. She's just a girl. Staggering after a butterfly. You can do this. Quit giving her the dead eyes. It's creepy. Even for a zombie.

Her skin glows more gray as the sun dances on her face. She's awesome. Better yet, I know it's a she unlike that hippie I tried to speak to earlier. Bonus points. I cannot take my eyes off of her, no matter how hard I try. If we had music, something from the 80's would be playing. I'm not sure what, but I know my parents always flooded the house with 80's music when I was human.
Something snaps me out of this trance as I continue to deadeye Anna as she staggers after the butterfly. It's Charlie. He's trying to pick up the trash that's under my foot. Sorry, man. I hobble over a step or two, and Charlie continues on with his trashfest. It's now or never, Edgar. Do something. Grunt something. Become Steve. Channel the cool that is Steve.

I wave and smile at Anna. She looks my way as the butterfly zips into the azure. Holy crap. This is happening. This is a thing, and I am part of it. She staggers my way. My smile widens. A tooth or two falls out as I do so, but that's okay. Chicks dig scars. Hopefully, they also dig a few less teeth. She is right in front of me. Play it cool. Say something smooth. I can smell her putrid breath in front of my face, but clearly if I can't get pizza anywhere, breath mints are more than likely out of the question as well. No problem. I can work with this. She tilts her head curiously. We make eye contact, and she reaches out her hand to touch my arm.

This. Is. Awesome.

My arm is still up in the waving position, and her hand works its way up to where my hand would have normally been.

CRAP. THE ONE TIME I THOUGHT A GIRL WAS FINALLY INTERESTED IN ME, I HAVE BEEN TOO DUMB TO NOTICE THAT I HAVE BEEN WAVING MY STUMP AT HER LIKE ONE OF THE BIGGEST MORONS IN HISTORY. AWESOME. SCORE THUS FAR, GIRLS—8,000, EDGAR—0.

I lower my arm. She grunts and staggers away slowly, grunting now only to herself. I would assume she's pissed now because her butterfly is nowhere around anymore. I search for reassurance. Steve is leaning against a building and staring off into space. I can't stress how cool this guy looks. If there were a fashion model magazine for zombies, Steve would be the guy on the cover every time. Charlie has made it to the end of the street with an armful of trash and appears to be searching for a trashcan to put them in. The only one looking my way is Loudmouth. Loudmouth with his missing jaw looks exactly how I feel right about now.
Even with the social gaffe of being Edgar the Stump Waver and the further humiliation of Charlie coming back and mistaking my recently fallen teeth for trash, I feel a brief kinship with these people.

Definitely with Anna. My gaze returns to her as she has currently mistaken a couple of wasps for her butterfly, and she has been stung a few times for it. You would think she would learn, but she keeps going back, and they keep stinging her. It doesn't matter. I could watch her all day long and never be bored with it. I know that sounds creepy, but I don't mean it that way at all.

I look around at my newly acquired friends. Charlie the groundskeeper, Steve the cover model, Loudmouth the jaw misser, and Anna. Sweet, beautiful, gray face illuminated in the sun and a little puffy from numerous wasp stings Anna.

We all decided we would stay in town for the night. I'm sure my woods community will probably wonder where I am and why I haven't called, but it just feels right staying here with these other zombies for the night. Maybe I can introduce them to what is left of Greg. Share some Greg stories and drywall sandwich recipes with them. The sun slowly descends in the western sky, and we all continue to pace in our respected circles until we see the sun again tomorrow.

4.

THE SUN rose, and it was our time to go scavenging around the town for whatever it was we were looking for. Steve had already been at it, and found a pair of shades that were missing a lens, and he put them on and took his spot up against the wall to be cool. Dammit, Steve. Being cool is a 24 hour job, but you totally kill it. Charlie was on street sweeping duty, and Loudmouth was going to work on a piece of candy he had found from some shop. Watching Loudmouth eat candy (or anything for that matter) is truly a work of art. He throws his head back, and grinds whatever he is eating on his top teeth and frantically swallows at the same time so whatever falls around his throat will get to his belly. I watch, entranced with the entire process..

I feel a cold hand placed upon my shoulder. It's Anna. I lean back. Big mistake. As she puts her weight on my shoulder, it makes me fall to the ground. I don't think anyone notices, so I work my way back to my fully upright position. She grunts, and I think it's an apology. At least that's what I think.. For all I know, she could have been calling me a loser. I don't think so, though. We make brief eye contact, and she staggers across the street into what used to be a gas station. The harmonious sounds of Loudmouth working on his candy fill the air, and I hobble after Anna.

The gas station looks like everywhere else. There are some shelves where food used to be, a couple of bathrooms that humans just opted not to flush, and the incessant humming of the overhead lights. Pretty standard. Anna is across the station and is attempting to look at herself in the reflection of where the drinks used to be. A withering hand pulls the mass of strings away from her face, and they fall back down. I look at my foot, and notice there's a small hair clip. I teeter delicately to pick it up, and hobble softly over to where Anna is standing. The hair clip has one of those pink bows on it that little girls would always wear. She's already beautiful to me without it, but I think it would at least be a decent gesture. As I approach, I try to get her attention like a normal human would. It sounds a little like this:

Aaaarrnnnuuughaaannnaaauh.

She turns around, and I hand the hair clip to her. She smiles, and clips it low on her hair. It falls out a couple of times, but she finally manages to make it hold on.

Sure, it utterly defeats the purpose of keeping the hair out of her face, but it brings to her a more feminine aspect. She turns from her reflection and shuffles away and I watch the pink bow dangling in the breeze. I follow her out into the brilliant sunshine. It's just been a moment. We were literally in there for just a small moment, and what do I see? Loudmouth. His cheekbones are almost touching his eye sockets, so I know he's trying to grin at both of us. Seriously? Can't a guy just be decent to a girl without someone grinning like a doofus at him?

Nope. Not even in the world of zombies can that happen. I bet Loudmouth is going to try and tell the other guys that Anna and I were in the gas station together. Really, that's the last thing I need now is some type of rumor floating about concerning me and Anna.

We all start to make our way to where Steve is still being cool up against a wall. We made it about halfway when it began to rain.

Normally, this would not be a big thing if we were, you know, *human*. The problem with being a zombie is that your skin rots the older you get. Any injury that is sustained doesn't go away. You probably have scars, right? When a zombie gets cut, it doesn't heal. The wound opens more and more over time. Add that lovely facet of our lives plus water, and you get the picture. Too much water turns what is left of our flesh to the consistency of Jell-O. Not very terrifying, is it? We all take shelter in the building that Steve has been holding up with the power of his coolness for a while.

This building was like any other grocery store you have ever been in. More ransacked shelves, cash registers, a break room, a manager's office—you get the idea. For Charlie, it was as close to heaven as he had ever been. So much to clean up! Charlie went to work immediately. Steve found his spot on the other side of the wall and stayed there again. Never even once took his shades off. Dammit, Steve. Even cool inside a building. Is there NO end to your smooth ways, good sir?

Anna started moving towards what would have been the candy aisle, and Loudmouth just kind of vanished. I know he was with us when we went in—every zombie knows that rain and us don't mix. It's funny. I always never minded the rain, but I would always hear people talk about how they would melt if they were in the rain for too long because of how sweet they were. If that holds true, then zombies are the sweetest people you've ever met. I make it down the frozen section in a vain attempt to try and find a pizza. Any pizza. It could be half thawed and soggy for all I care at this point. I would still eat it. Just for a taste of normalcy, as the only people who are trying to "rebuild society" at this point are a bunch of nutjobs with way too much ammo at their immediate disposal.

I'm checking all the cases. Nothing. Emptiness.

Oh, there's some steamed broccoli that has been the subject of some condensation issues, but I think I would rather watch Loudmouth attempt to give someone CPR than ingest that garbage. I continue my path. Anna has turned down the aisle that I am on.

Sparks fly in my mind. I can't shake how undeniably gorgeous she is. Her sunken eyes. Her exposed nasal cavities. The way that little bow dangles playfully from her hair in a desperate attempt to hang on. I wave this time with the arm that my hand is connected to still. She smiles. If she had better functions of her reflex system, I know she would be blushing. I just know it. If there were birds in here, they would be surrounding her like the corpse of Cinderella and singing left and right.

I take one step towards her.

She returns the favor.

I take another step.

She staggers towards me coquettishly.

There is this high pierced screeching over the speakers. Microphone feedback, I would assume. She covers her ears. I cover my ear. Silence for a second, and then like thunder over the store's broadcast system:

"GNAOURAPHGRONNNINUHMAUPHRO! NUHCUGHNENAUOPHUH!"

It would seem Loudmouth has found the manager's office and decided to either give orders to someone, or inform us of the great values in the seafood section today. Hard to tell which when all Loudmouth can speak in is guttural utterances. And now the brainiac thinks he is the manager of this grocery store. Fantastic.

I turn my back on Anna as I hear a noise. At the end of the aisle, I see a dim silhouette of Charlie heading towards another aisle pushing a mop and a bucket as he grumbles to himself.

These are my people, folks. A dimwit missing a jaw barking orders to a neurotic neat freak while the zombie of Lou Reed hangs out at the front of the store.
And of course, my dearest dilapidating Anna. My mind wanders as I turn back to face her so we can eventually be near each other.

And she's gone. Poof. No Anna. Nothing. I start to head down the aisle to catch up with her so that we can creep and hobble towards each other again. I know what you're thinking. How could I possibly be that infatuated with a woman I had just met yesterday? Look. If you think for a second that dating in the human world is difficult, try being a zombie for five seconds. Before the outbreak, you guys could install an app on your phone, or your tablet, or your dog (exaggerating. Sort of.), make a couple of swipes, and bing! Instant love! Even if there was technology available for us to use in this world we are in right now, what in the world would the app users *look like*? Can you imagine what Loudmouth's profile picture would be? Charlie would be too busy cleaning to upload a photo, and Steve would be too cool to take one. It would be an absolute mess. I wasn't that great at selfies to begin with, and I would more than likely be even worse at it with only one hand left.

I turn the corner. Still, no Anna. Go down another aisle, same thing.

I move as quickly as I can down the aisles. I am every dad who has ever went to the grocery store and has no idea where anything is. I go up to the front of the store. Steve is still being cool up against the wall. Dammit, Steve.

I find the manager's office, and Loudmouth has found an official short sleeve white collar shirt with a name tag that reads: "No Matter What You Gave, It's Great to Save!" Not only is that the most asinine slogan I have ever read, but Loudmouth is trying to bark orders at me like I work there. He even gestured frantically towards the time clock. Sorry, boss. I'll try to be more punctual next time WHEN WE'RE BOTH ACTUALLY HUMAN AND BOTH EMPLOYED BY THIS PARTICULAR FACILITY. I leave Loudmouth to his railings.

I find Charlie, and attempt to see if he knows where Anna went to. Something is wrong. I have a feeling about it in my bones. Charlie just stares at me and mops under where my foot would have been previously. Charlie is about as helpful as the others, so I continue my scan of the store. She's not in here. That's just not possible. She was just there. I get to the back of the store where the stockrooms are, and I notice there's an open door. I head towards it, and I see a car with something struggling in the backseat of it. The car speeds away, and I look down to find Anna's hair clip in the dust.

Time freezes for a moment.

The only thing I can seem to determine is that somehow, someway, someone has captured Anna. The only thing I notice about the car as it speeds away is that there are two stickers on the back glass. One states rather proudly that their child is an honor student, and the other is that silly stick figure zombie family. You know the one I'm talking about? Like the mom, the dad, the two kids, and the cat and dog are all zombies?

Stop doing this, humans. There's nothing cool about being a zombie. Nothing. Everyone wants to kill you, the communication levels are low at best, your body slowly rots, and rain is a constant concern. Why would you trade being human for this? I promise you, it's not glorious. I know that was Anna in the backseat. I just know it.

And I know I have to find her.

It's time. It's time to stop being an unrelenting weenie for once in my life, and become the Edgar I know that dwells within me. This is one of those moments that begin movies. I walk out of the stockroom, and Loudmouth is still blaring over the intercom. It must be a labor dispute by now because Charlie has thrown down his bucket and is yelling back at the intercom. This, of course, doesn't seem to slow down Loudmouth in the slightest. I guess it's true. Give a moron a title, and they'll swear they're the center of the universe.

I grab Charlie by the shoulder and hobble up to the front where I remove Loudmouth from his once glorious throne. He refuses to remove the white collared shirt, nor the name tag. We all make our way past Steve, and Steve peels himself from the wall and attempts to snap his fingers. When he does, a little of the skin and muscle of his thumb comes off. Steve just glances at it, and gives us a partial thumbs up featuring an exposed thumb bone. Dammit, Steve.

We make our way out of the building and get around to the back where the car pulled off. The tracks are fairly fresh in the gravel, but after about thirty yards of it, they turn on to the road. The good news is that they appear to be turning left, so left we shall go.

For me.

For Anna.

For pizza.

5.

WALKING DOWN whatever paved streets are left as a zombie really sucks. If you've ever walked in uncomfortable shoes, you know the searing pain that radiates through every nerve ending and fiber of your being. Take that same idea and add really spongy flesh that has a knack for sliding off when it comes into contact with any remotely abrasive surface in a society that shoes are a rarity at all, and that's what it feels like for a zombie to walk on asphalt. The stump where my foot used to be is slowly grinding to the consistency of raw hamburger meat. Smells a bit like it as well. I hobble off to the side of the road where the dirt is a little more pleasant and my compatriots follow after.

It would seem that I am somehow the leader of this troop. Even Steve is slinking behind me. Every time I turn around to look back at them all, Steve responds with a tilted smile and a half off thumbs up, and Loudmouth and Charlie are still engaged in their heated labor disputes, but they're following me nonetheless.

I try to think back to a time when I was ever a leader of anything. I've *never* been one. I was always the kid in school whose scores on every test were just average. I'm not even saying that to be modest at all. My first year of middle school—actually—every year of school when they started giving actual grades was usually between a 75 and an 80. Even when I got to high school, I thought if I got involved in the school, I would surround myself with more driven students, and that would get me driven as well. I joined every club available and dropped out after two weeks from every club I joined. Even when I graduated from my school, I was literally the name in the middle of all the students who were called. I'm pretty sure my mom clapped, but apart from that, crickets.

And now, here I am. Leading. On a quest. Get the girl, get some pizza. Happily ever after and all that. My faithful companions behind me, the open road in front of us.

Well, not totally open. If there's one thing that the zombie shows did get pretty accurate, it's the amount of abandoned cars that just litter any road you try to walk down. Not only is it really unattractive, it's just outright annoying. Even if I wanted to get to the other side of the road, it would take me the better part of an hour to do so due to the auto graveyard that blocks my route. And why did they abandon their cars? Were they just tired of sitting in traffic, or when the outbreak hit, did they just suddenly decide that now would be the great time to fulfill their lifelong dream of going off the grid and just bailed? That's also the thing that's kind of pissing me off about Anna being taken by the honor student zombie family—where in the world did they get the gas for their car? Gas is finite—just like those hunters I encountered earlier, their ammo is finite. You might have killed Greg, but you're not going to kill us all. That's not how any of this works.

What's more, I don't know *why* they took her at all. Are they just some science nerds who believe they can somehow find a cure for being a zombie? Did they think they needed some sass to add to the zombie family sticker they had? Are they just planning to butcher her for their own amusement? I can't think of that now. I have to remain focused.

The benefit to the roads being blocked is that any cars that are still functioning, we can see where they drive off the roads and we can use this bit of information to our advantage as they make more tracks for us to follow. We continue on our path. As long as we can see tracks, that's where we'll keep moving.

We walk for the better portion of the day, and I'm starting to wonder if this will ever happen. Any of it. Anna, the pizza, the happy ever after. It just seems like such a struggle. Even if we could drive any of these cars that are right beside us, I'm sure it would be Loudmouth wanting to drive. God knows he would drive it for ten feet straight into a tree. I can't drive with the whole missing foot thing, there's not a car clean enough for Charlie to even consider getting in to, and Steve would most likely just lean up against the thing and be cool as we tried to drive off. I hear leaves crunching in the woods, and I stop. They're heavier than animal footsteps and a lot less deliberate than zombie footsteps. We all stop.

Steve thumbs in the direction of the noise, and we all take cover behind some abandoned cars to wait it out. If it is a hunter, and there's more than one, this adventure of The Rotting Ramblers is about to end rather quickly. Best to be still and make no sudden movements. The footsteps come to a halt pretty close to our location.

Either something (or someone) has seen us, or thinks they have seen something.. The footsteps come closer. Whatever it is, it's attempting to muffle the sound of it's footsteps. Usually not a good sign if you're a zombie. From where I am, I can see Steve and Loudmouth. Steve gives me the bony thumbs up, and Loudmouth is too occupied with his name tag on his shirt to notice me at all. I can't see Charlie at all, but I would imagine that wherever he is, he is cleaning the road around him quite well.

The footsteps come closer. I hear the sound of something like metal being moved around. It has to be a hunter. From my brief experience with them, nothing moves like a zombie hunter. Audible for a second, and silent as a breeze the next. I hear what must be the muzzle of his gun scraping slowly against one of the cars. The sound becomes louder as he approaches closer to where I am. If I make a sound, he'll hear me. More than likely, he'll probably kill me. Which sucks because I'm a pretty good guy once you get to know me. I start to shake. I can't help it. Yeah, being a zombie has its disadvantages, but I don't want to die. Please walk past me, man. Please. If the outbreak never happened, I would have been the kid who served you your fancy coffee. I would have never misspelled your name on the cup, and we would be so cool that I would slide you my employee discount just because I thought you were a good person. I close my eyes. I don't want to see this. I don't want my last sight on earth to be a man who is trying to kill me. I just want to find Anna. And pizza. That's it, man. Just let me go. Just let me— And then I hear another noise. Out of nowhere, this sound like someone dropped a rock on top of one of the numerous cars happens. I hear this guy's boots crunch as he turns around, and he empties everything he has out of the magazine in his gun. Hot brass falls on my arms. It burns, but I just brush it off. The footsteps go away and head in the direction of where the noise came from. When the footsteps stop, I then hear another noise. This one is hard to describe, but in the comic books I used to read, when someone was hit with an object, there was usually the word thud attached to it, so we'll go with that. It was a thud.

Steve and I stand up to check out the scene. Loudmouth eventually becomes less enamored with his name tag and joins in. What we see before us is nothing short of the most badass thing we have ever seen. It's Charlie. Holding a branch. And standing over an unconscious hunter. The same one that was going to kill all of us if he had found us.

The clearest thing that I can put together is that whatever car Charlie was hiding behind must have had something heavy and he threw is to make the noise and distract the hunter. That's what I want to believe. More than likely, Charlie was trying to clean up rocks in our path that we had walked over and was looking for a place to dispose of them properly. I know it probably killed Charlie to throw that rock and just put more litter out, but I'm glad he did. Now, one of the bigger problems we have on our hands is that we have a knocked out hunter who will be coming to pretty soon, and now he's going to be a little upset about Charlie knocking him upside the head. Steve slowly rummages through one of the cars and finds some jumper cables, and Loudmouth follow suit. After eight or nine cars, we have enough jumper cables to be able to give a jump to someone in the next state. I don't know whose cars these are, but they were over-prepared for any dead battery scenario you could imagine. I pat the guy down and take his weapons away the best that I can with one hand. No sooner do I do this, Charlie starts to pick them up and sets them in a neat pile away from the guy.

I would say the guy is in his mid-thirties. He's dressed in enough tactical gear to keep most soldier of fortune online retailers blush. Even his socks read "tactical". Why? Just why? They're socks, G.I. Joke. Nothing is tactical about socks. Nothing. He also has a gut that seemingly every father gets after they have children. It's almost like a reverse pregnancy. The wife has a child and her stomach gets smaller after the birth, and the father's stomach gets *bigger* after the birth. By the looks of his sunglasses, I can only determine he is one of those fathers that yells at his kid to keep his focus during a t-ball game while his kid is in left field wearing a glove on his head and turning in circles. I take them off of him. Yep. Even has the shades tan lines. His vest he is wearing catches my eye the most, however. There's a couple of patches on it. One reads Zombie Response Crew (charming), and the other patch shows a zombie stick family.

Exactly like the sticker on the car they took Anna in.

This must be a thing, and this guy must be part of it somehow. I can't imagine every human has this lame sense of humor left. If it is, then I grow more proud of my zombie status with every fleeting moment of my life. Bad humor, more inflated sense of self than when this whole thing started, and this sickening hate for everything that isn't them.

Steve and Loudmouth nudge me to the side, and drag the guy to the nearest tree. They take the jumper cables and tie him to it. True to form, Steve is doing all the work with tying him up, and Loudmouth is supervising. I mean, Loudmouth does have the shirt for it, I suppose. Eventually, the guy comes to, and starts screaming at the top of his lungs for someone to come and help. Charlie comes to where we are, and we all stand around this guy who is screaming like a maniac. I guess if I wasn't a zombie, this scene would be pretty intense. He's surrounded by four zombies and we are all looking down and staring at him. I'm sure he thinks we're going to eat him, but honestly I think we're more relieved than anything about not getting killed ourselves. He stops for a minute and then starts babbling about how he has a family. We just all look at each other. We have no idea how to communicate with this guy. None. Even if we did speak, all he would hear is grunts and groans. Steve leaves us and begins rummaging through some other cars. This draws the man's attention and now he's pleading with us not to torture him.

Not torture you? How many zombie apocalypse videos did you watch before this outbreak started, dude? Who has EVER heard of zombies torturing people? Steve comes back to us. He is holding an old pen in one hand, and a crumpled up receipt in another hand. He put the receipt up against the tree, and attempts to write a message to this guy, and leans down to hold it front of his face. I see this bewildered look come across the guy's face, but he's not panicking anymore and has shut up about his family. Steve turns back around to all of us, and shows us what the note reads. I make out the following words:

NAHT. CEWL.

What Steve has in coolness, he lacks in literacy. Steve, Charlie, and Loudmouth start to turn away. Steve left the note in the guy's lap, and I'm assuming he knew what it read. I stay there with him for a few moments longer. I know the guy has just had the living crap scared out of him, but honestly, I don't care. Had it not been for Charlie's obsessive cleanliness and quick thinking, he would have killed us all, returned to wherever his people were and bragged about it all night over cheap beer like some kind of low budget Beowulf. I want him to know how displeased I am with the whole wanting to kill us situation. I want to know where Anna is. I want to know that she's okay. I still want pizza. I want a lot of things, and you, sir, are impeding our progress. I do the only thing I know to do to let this guy know how much I dislike him. I flip him off dead in his face. The same look of confusion is on the man's face, and it is at that time that I take notice that I have not flipped him off at all, but rather just raised my stump in his face.

Take that, sir. Stump you for trying to kill us before you even get to know us. Steve was right about you. Not cool at all. Not. Cool. Steve picks up some of the hunter's weapons, and Charlie takes the rest. Loudmouth is protesting that he doesn't get any weapons, but that's all for the best that he doesn't. Loudmouth with weapons would be like the drunken dads on the 4th of July who insist that dipping mortars into gasoline would be "awesome". Bad. Idea. I don't know why Steve and Charlie pick up the weapons, but maybe any hunters we encounter from here on will think twice when they see zombies with weapons. Probably not, but we can always hope.

6.

IF I haven't mentioned it before, walking as a zombie sucks. It takes forever when you're alone, and when you're in a group, it makes it a little harder than it would normally be. Picture a class of kindergartners getting ready to go to recess, and with every step they take, there are people that come out of nowhere offering shiny things and cotton candy. Most zombies have really bad attention deficit issues, and because of it, we're too distracted to get much of anything done. Take me, for example. I'm not above it at all. Even prior to all of this happening, my mind would wander constantly. I guess that's the way it is with most people who are into art, but I'm always looking at something and picturing what else it could be. I remember one night my mom had made tacos for dinner, and as I sat down, I started staring at my taco. Suddenly in my mind, the taco became a naval ship. The SS Hardshell. Logically, I became the sea monster Dordandatron about to send the Hardshell down to Davy Jones' locker. I thought I was making the noises inside of my head of the endless seas of screaming from the sailors aboard when after I lowered my taco from my face, my mom and dad had this look of utter horror on their faces. I smiled at them with strings of shredded cheese hanging from my lip. They both shook their heads and we continued our meal in silence.

Then again, I was always kind of a weird kid. Maybe the weird kids were more susceptible to the virus when it first hit. Maybe we were too weird to be human anymore. Being normal kind of bothered me, though. I would go outside, and all of our houses looked the same. People would wave and smile at each other as they drove by or walked by, but then you always heard them talking crap about how someone's lawn looked or some salacious detail about someone having an affair with someone else. Fake. Always fake. With zombies, you at least know what you're in for. It's kind of hard to be pretentious when at any moment, you could sneeze and an ear could fall off.

We continued down the road until it got dark, and then it was time for rest. We found a nice clump of trees that provided a pretty good canopy in case it rained. Steve found the biggest tree to lean his back against and watched the rest of us pace through his one eyed shades, and Charlie cleaned out a small spot for him to pace in. Loudmouth found a spot where the weeds were slightly high, so he thought it would be really funny whenever Charlie or I paced by to crouch down in the weeds and reach out and grab our ankles in an attempt to scare us. We spent the majority of the evening listening to his muffled laughter whenever he thought he did. When the sun came up, we started on our voyage again.

The good thing is that nothing of note happened that day. We spent the day taking our time and following the tracks wherever we thought they lead. There were no hunters, no animals, nothing. Every now and then you could hear birds singing, but that was about it. It was a nice day, all things considered.

As we made our way down the road, we came to where a split happened. I always hated the term "fork in the road". The only thing I see in my head when someone says that is this discarded eating utensil all sad and alone. Probably missing his brother knife and sister spoon. Spoon and knife probably filed a missing utensil report with the local kitchen police. Fork was no doubt on the back of every milk carton all around the world. Shirts were made to raise awareness of fork's disappearance, there was an album made for fork and all proceeds of the sale went to spoon and knife's family until fork made his triumphant return back to 137 Kitchen Drawer Lane where they could be one happy set again.
See what I mean? No focus. At least on the trivial things. Anna and pizza? That's not trivial at all.

The tracks seemed to go left, so that is where we followed. We hobbled and crept for what had to be at least seven or eight miles. Probably more. It's hard to tell when I'm thumping along as fast as I can lead and everyone else staggering behind me. I've been mostly looking at my foot and my stump of my leg to try to avoid as many tree roots as possible. While the dirt is treating my stump much better than the asphalt would, even the slightest incline or decline in the dirt is a potential hazard, We stop for a second, and I look up. There's an abandoned electronics store that's pretty ran down from the outside, so I can only imagine the comforts that lie within. The weeds cover half the side of the building, and the shop itself looks likes it was a precursor of things to come before there were any zombies of note. We head that way to go and check and see if there are any clues that would help us with Anna's whereabouts.

Okay, so we're not the greatest detectives known to mankind. Even if they DID stop there, what in the world would they be looking for? The dust that covers these console televisions is about three inches thick, and there's cobwebs everywhere inside. It's so dirty that I see Charlie about to be in the throes of a full on panic attack. The pace of his grunting has accelerated, and he is starting to almost flap his arms with the hope that he can get enough wind generated to somehow magically sweep the place clean. Steve has found another place on the wall to hold up, and Loudmouth is slamming his face into the dust on the televisions to try and see if he can leave an imprint of his face afterwards. There's nothing really useable in here. We make our way back out and Charlie's grunting has slowed down slightly. It increases when he sees how dusty Loudmouth's face is, and Charlie pulls a scrap of paper off the ground in order to rectify the situation. I look to my left and there's a light pole with a bunch of flyer stapled to it.

Needless to say, I'm the only one of us that doesn't have the literacy skills of a drooling two year old child, so I make my way over to it. It's a bunch of the exact same flyer, and it reads something like this:

ALIVE? WANT TO STAY THAT WAY? JOIN THE ZOMBIE
RESPONSE CREW! FOLLOW THE ARROWS TWO MILES
FROM THIS EXACT LOCATION! FOOD AND DRINKS
PROVIDED! HOT DOGS AND PONY RIDES FOR THE KIDS!
YOU'RE ALMOST THERE!

Okay, wait. Pony rides? These weekend warrior assclowns have
PONIES? *And* kids? Great. Stupendous. I can just imagine what
anti-zombie hate propaganda they're filling these kids' heads with.
These poor kids. They'll never get to know what good people
zombies are. What happened to humanity? We used to be able to at
least tolerate each other's existence, and now if you're not human,
you're the enemy instantly. I guess when more people started to turn
to zombies people started to realize that they actually needed each
other instead of trying to destroy each other every fifteen seconds.
Hey. You're welcome, humans. Sincerely, everyone who has ever
been turned into a zombie.

I call my crew over, and gesture towards the sign in an attempt to
explain where we are heading, and what we will undoubtedly be
heading into. Steve looks like he gets it, Charlie is picking up scraps
of flyer that have fallen down, and Loudmouth's white collared shirt
is now gray from numerous faceplants into antiquated technology.
One of the stop signs up the road has an arrow that is pointing
forward, so forward we're going. We make it a little bit past the stop
sign, and a dog starts barking at us. Animals, for whatever reason,
seemed to have been immune to the disease, and therefore couldn't
become zombies. It's more than likely for the best, however. I can
only imagine that little dog my next door neighbor had turning into a
zombie. I hated that thing. Not that I hate animals. In fact, I'm quite
a fan, but this thing was unbridled hell in a two pound package. No
matter what you did or *didn't* do, this dog would try to attack you
with a quaking fervor for blood in its tiny little gums. Like any other
Southern suburban housewife, she gave it this horrendous name—
SugarBelle. I wanted to projectile vomit every time she would
bellow out in her front yard for this hellhound to come back to its
lair. I wouldn't be anywhere near the yard, and the damn thing
would run over and nip at the back of my heels.

The joke would be on SugarBelle now. I only have one heel to nip at any more. Score thus far, Edgar one, two pounds of four legged hatred, zero.

We all look at the dog, and it decides that it is in its best interest to leave us alone. I would like to think that its the ferocity of the way we look as zombies that petrified this canine, but more than likely it wasn't sure what to make of all of us. Can't understand why. I mean, we're just four zombies making our way in life. One's missing a jaw and wearing a manager's shirt. One has a rifle hanging from the back of his neck, one refuses to give up his half shades no matter where he is, and then there's me. The symmetrical amputee zombie. All of us going on a quest with no idea what we're going to do once we get there. Totally normal.

As the dogs trots away, I see Loudmouth looking at me. The expression on his face is one of longing after the dog ran away. You have to be kidding me. Loudmouth seriously wants a dog? He raises his arms towards where the dog was, and he starts crying. I mean, CRYING. If the hunters didn't know where we were, I'm pretty sure they have a good clue now. Loudmouth is openly sobbing, and you can see snot mixing with the drool that's coming down in sheets from his upper palette. Awesome. Apparently, Loudmouth is an animal lover, and the only thing that will console him is if the dog comes with us. Me, I just want to find Anna. And pizza.

7.

NEEDLESS TO say, it took some time to get the dog to have anything to do with us. Loudmouth had a small wound on his leg, and he pulled off some of his flesh off of it in an attempt to get the dog to come near us. At first, the dog hesitated, but after the utter futility of zombies trying to whistle for a dog to come, he relented and was our newest faithful companion.

It sounds fantastic, doesn't it? A zombie and his buddies plus their newly acquired canine companion on the path to rescue the fair but slowly rotting maiden from the evil clutches of the Zombie Response Crew? Allow me to explain what it really looks like. Because of Loudmouth's wonderful idea to feed the dog some of his homemade all organic zombie leg jerky, the dog has discovered quite a taste for it. In fact, the dog has permanently sank his teeth into Loudmouth's leg, and Loudmouth is dragging the dog along. Every now and then he stops and leans down to pet the dog which refuses to release his viselike grip on his leg. At least he's content, and we can start to make our way down the road. Slowly, but we're on our way.

The arrows that are directing us are pretty visible. I don't know if this tells us that wherever we're heading is a new establishment or they just have a lot of humans that would love nothing more in their life than to find us and kill us to preserve what they call society. My leg stump is starting to itch. More than likely, I'm starting to develop some type of infection. I can only imagine what Loudmouth is feeling with that furball mouth-stapled to his leg, but he doesn't seem to notice. In fact, I could swear he's trying to hum a song. I hear the rifle bouncing against Charlie's chest with every step he takes, and one of the weapons Steve must have taken from the hunter is a knife as he keeps twirling it every now and then. I don't want to think about what these jerks have in store for Anna, so I focus on my ultimate desire: pizza.

My love for pizza began when I was a little boy. Even back then, if I had the choice between breathing air and pizza, I would chosen pizza every time. One of the roadblocks that I would discover throughout my life is that some people have no clue how to pizza at all. I remember being invited to this kid Frankie Shack's birthday party when I was in third grade, and I wasn't excited about being invited, to tell the truth. After the fishstick fiasco with Eunice, it was social suicide to be seen talking to me, let alone be invited to a function that would undoubtedly be filled with my peers. *I* didn't even want to go. I think he must have told his mom about the beatdown in the lunchroom because when he handed me the invitation, he did it like I was some type of wounded animal he didn't want to get close to. I'm sure she made him invite me so I wouldn't feel left out.

What Frankie Shack conveniently forgot is that when we were all in first grade, we were out playing kickball and he had these gray sweatpants on. I guess he was too invested in playing right field to notice that he had to go pee, so he just figured he would open the floodgates all in those gray sweatpants of his. When in was time to switch sides, he just jogged in like there wasn't the entire contents of his bladder bleeding through his athletic apparel choice. When Shane Fitzsimmons pointed this out to anyone who couldn't see (or smell) what had happened with Frankie, inventor and CEO of the PantsOcean, Frankie looked at us all and said that he had fallen in a puddle when he ran out to play right field.

Fell in a puddle.

With just your crotch.

Got it, Frankie.

Anyway, Frankie's soiree centered around having pizza. Okay. I can handle hanging out with FrankieFluids, I thought. It wasn't like many people wanted to be friends with me in third grade anyway, so why not? How bad could it be? I went into Frankie's house and found a place to stand up against the wall. Not like Steve—I wasn't that cool. Frankie's mom came up to me and asked if I wanted a goody bag. I nodded awkwardly, and she handed me this cellophane wrapped bundle, and there was a cookie in it. I bite into it, realizing that the entire thing is made of oatmeal and raisins. I wanted to throw it at Frankie's mom, but she would tell my mom. I avoided the other "treats" in the bag and waited for the big show of pizza. Frankie's dad came in with what seemed an unending supply of pizza. I stared rapturously at the cardboard encasements as they passed by. The whiff of steam and the visions of small spots of grease under the boxes almost brought a tear to my small eye. It was glory in eight slices per box. Frankie's dad stacks them up, four boxes in each stack. All the kids at Frankie's party lined up, and I was waiting in the back with my paper plate in hand. I couldn't see the pizza too well until I got up to the table.

My smile went away. Quickly. One stack is nothing but mushroom pizza, and the other stack is every vegetable known to man minus mushrooms. My lip started quivering, and I couldn't stop it from happening. I started to cry. Like, ugly crying. My plate drifted softly to the floor after I dropped it, and this drew the attention of Frankie's parents quickly. They tried to console me, only to find that I was inconsolable. They called my mom, and she picked me up. I didn't stop crying about that incident at Frankie's almost until my bedtime. It was possibly the biggest tragedy of my life up to that point. If the tragedies had stopped then, I would have had a more decent go at life.

If only.

Look at you. You're turning up your nose and placing judgment as to how third grade me reacted towards Frankie and his family's earthy pizza choices. I can feel it. Know what? That's your opinion. Let me tell you mine. Order a pizza from a store. Get it however you want it. Wait until it's delivered to your house. When it gets there, find someone who is suffering from athlete's foot, and scrape their fungus on your pizza. No? Doesn't sound good, does it? So one form of fungus is "acceptable" to put on pizza, but another isn't? When you're eating mushrooms in or on ANYTHING, you're consuming fungus. Vegetables? They grow from the earth. Same place as that fungus you're chewing on. Trees grow from the earth as well. Why not put some tree bark on your next order and get to chomping down on that? I bet you can just taste the nutrients from that tree bark special. Some people just don't know how to pizza. Put meat on the pizza. Consume. Be happy. Pretty simple, really.

I snap out of my internal rant and turn around to make sure everyone is still following me. They are, but Charlie and Loudmouth have stopped a few feet behind me. Steve turns around and we both watch the scene that is unfolding behind us. Loudmouth has figured that it now would be a wonderful time to try and teach his attached dog how to fetch. He is picking up sticks and throwing them for the dog, but the only one who is going after them is Charlie as he must be thinking that Loudmouth is littering and it is just another mess for him to clean up. The dog has yet to break his grasp on Loudmouth's leg. I groan and turn back around to follow the arrows and everyone else takes the hint.

Eventually, we get to an arrow that points right. We try to look down the street where it's pointing the best we can, but the road seems to stretch to infinity. It's a dirt road, and it looks like it is completely clear of any broken down cars. On one hand, that's a good sign that there will be no interference from impromptu auto graveyards as we make our way down the road. On the other hand, it's too clear. Whoever made this road must have made it with the purpose that they can also see as far as we can down it. We begin our trek down the road. I decide that would still be better walking in the woods on the side of the road in case there's any humans heading down anytime soon.

We're about halfway down the road, and I start to be able to make out a picture of this place. It's pretty much sheet metal and wooden beams surrounding it with barbwire on the top of the place. The reason for the barbwire eludes me, though. Are they trying to keep us out, or keep themselves in? If they're trying to keep us out, the high sheet metal would be effective enough. It's not like zombies are these incredible pole-vaulters that are looking to clear 14 foot walls with our trusty skills or anything. As a matter of fact, more than likely even if we could attempt to do it, we would lose limbs on the way up. I lost two just trying to squeeze out of a door and run for crying out loud. I don't think pole vaulting will be in any of our futures anytime soon. We continue towards this impromptu fortress and there are two humans with rifles on either side of what must be a gate to enter the town. They have the same shades on as the guy we met earlier. Was there a sale on those shades, and the leader of this community thought that this look would be intimidating? There are a few cars parked outside of the fort, and they all have the same stickers as the car that took Anna from me.

Okay, from us. But still.

We all pause in the woods. Steve takes his shade off. Charlie stops chasing sticks. The dog on Loudmouth's leg stops growling and looks up. The two humans that are keeping watch are doing a terrible job of it. One is almost asleep, and the other looks to be texting someone. Who in the world is he texting? Is he just rummaging through his contact list to see who all is still human? Furthermore, *what* would he be texting? Is he all: "Hey, Sandra. Wanna come over? Post apocalypse and chill?" He holds his phone up a couple of times and lowers it back down again. Is he looking for a signal? Do cell phones even work anymore? Is he—

Oh god.

He's taking selfies.

Are you serious? There are zombies all over the world that you and your jacked-up pickup crew are wanting to slaughter en masse, mister hard-to-kill Johnny Tacti-cool and you're taking more selfies than a narcissistic thirteen year old cheerleader? Who are you sending them to? Is social media still up and running? Everything regarding what we knew as civilization has been annihilated except social media? If it is, I guess that answers the question of what would be left if a country dropped the bomb, and apparently it would be roaches and social media.

Nope. He's taking selfies. I've never been one to use the word hate, but I think I hate this guy. He's now leaning over the edge of the platform he's on. I guess he's trying to show off his rifle, shades, and how high up off the ground he is. I hope he drops the phone and it hits him in his stupid face. I turn to look over at St—

Wait. Where's Steve? Loudmouth, his attached life form, and Charlie all seem to be walking away from where I am, and they're following Steve, who has moved cautiously towards the edge of the woods to get closer to the fort. I hobble after them, and I'm trying to get Steve's attention. This is a bad idea. Even if Anna is in there, we have no way to get inside. They'll gun us down before I can even see her. Before I can even find pizza again. Steve makes it to one of the cars closest to the gate, and we all follow and crouch down. I'm trying to put this all together. Why is Steve going closer to the place where the humans are WHO WANT TO WIPE US OFF THE FACE OF THE PLANET. Steve puts back on his shade and holds a rotting hand up telling us to wait here. He makes his move when the guard lowers his phone again. I peer cautiously around the car. Please, Steve. Please be careful. If they find you, they'll find us. I look, and Steve is about five feet from the base of the guard tower. He has one hand on his hip, one hand is holding up two fingers close to his shade, and he is attempting to do the duck face with whatever is left of his lips. He remains in this position until the guard holds his phone up for another selfie.

Ladies and gentlemen, meet Steve. The zombie photo-bomber. Hashtag no filter. Hashtag zombie life. Hashtag woke up like this. Dammit, Steve. As the guard lowers his phone to look at his Mona Selfie, he notices Steve's tomfoolery in the background. This of course results in a hail of bullets straight down towards Steve's general vicinity. We all panic, and all of us make it back to the woods as quickly as possible. The leaves crumble beneath my stump, and I can hear voices. Some of them sound a little like the ones who killed Greg, but when you're a zombie, human voices all start to sound a little similar after a while. They're chasing us. I know they are. Hide, Edgar. Find a place for everyone to hide. The deeper we run into the woods, the fewer voices I can hear. A couple of shots whiz past my head, but that's about as close as they get to hitting us.

We all fall down in a big zombie pile amongst the leaves, and Steve starts pulling leaves over us in order for us to hide from whoever is chasing us. I hear footsteps like I did from the first hunter. Only now, I hear more of them. I would imagine there are about three of them, but I can't be sure. We're all huddled together under this pile, and the smell is less than pleasant, but we're alive. One of the voices yells to the other humans that he has found something. They come to where we are. It's like I'm having déjà vu. They ask each other repeatedly what that is, and I have no idea what they're talking about. I think we're pretty well camouflaged, and the next thing I know, I hear a growling and barking accompanied with the sounds of the men running away quickly. I know Loudmouth was laying on his side under our leaf blanket, and from the men's perspective, they must have seen this dog balancing on his nose on top of a pile of leaves. A weird image, I'll admit. Pretty sure I would have tried to figure out what it was as well. Apparently they got a little too close to the all-you-can-eat Loudmouth buffet, and the dog took exception to their presence. Good boy! Good boy! Who's a good boy? You are! We hear the men in the distance screaming to open the gate, and then we no longer hear their voices. We wait for a little while, and the dog returns to Loudmouth and attaches himself back to his leg. It's not the most glorious self defense in the history of the world, but it's pretty effective, I have to confess.

8.

WE STAYED in our safe spot in the woods for a few days. They
didn't bother to send more people out to look for us, and we had no
real desire to go and give them another photo-zomb. We watched the
road and the fort as best we could—checking to see if there were
patterns of people coming and going, seeing what cars and trucks
might come down the road. Apart from the guards in those two
posts, you would think that the entire Zombie Response Crew was
made up of about four people total. At night, we would go around
the perimeter to find a place that was open, or even had bad
construction so we could squeeze through, but the past few days
showed us absolutely nothing. Yes, Charlie cleaned up the brass that
fell from them shooting at us, but apart from those trashy treasures,
there wasn't much to speak of.

And one day, we saw our spot. It was a smaller delivery truck that
came up to the gate, but it had this pull down door that either wasn't
or couldn't be pulled down all the way. There was a two and a half
foot gap between that pull down door and the floor of the truck. The
truck pulled up, honked three times, and the gate slowly opened for
it.

That's our ticket. That's how we get in. That's how we save Anna
and get back to living a normal zombie life and look for pizza in
peace. One small caveat with my plan, however: I have o clue how
we're going to stop that truck if and when it comes back. Doesn't
matter. I call Steve over to me by waving my stump in a beckoning
fashion, and he sees what I see. Apparently he approves as the bony
thumbs up surfaces. Loudmouth and Charlie make it over and we
gesture towards the plan. Charlie is with the plan, but Loudmouth
objects and starts pointing frantically towards his name tag. Steve
slaps him upside the back of his head, and Loudmouth gets with the
plan. Sorry, boss. We're not in a grocery store anymore.

I pace more than usual that night. It's not uncommon for zombies to randomly pace, but when I'm thinking of saving my love, I pace so much that there is a miniature dirt tack that I have created by dawn's breaking. How to stop that delivery truck if it comes back? How? If we go out in the road, they'll see us and run us over. None of us know how to use the two weapons we have at our immediate disposal, and even if Charlie shot the gun, he would dislocate his shoulder after one pull of the trigger. We need to get in that truck.

The idea of getting in that truck consumes me. It's all I think about. About a week later, I hear that same engine the truck has from far off down the dirt road. I get excited. This is it. How to stop the truck? How? Steve is leaning up against a tree with a constant thumbs up— that's been his position for as long as I have grunted to him about the plan. Charlie is organizing the leaves by color and size in a recently cleared spot of dirt, and Loudmouth is petting that psycho dog of his. I don't get what it is with Loudmouth and that dog. Yeah, he scared those hunters away with his exorcist-like standing on his nose, but he just came back and re-attached to his leg.

It hits me then.

Loudmouth's leg.

I hobble over to where Loudmouth is petting his dog. Loudmouth looks up at me and has this confused look on what is left of his face. Not totally uncommon for Loudmouth to be confused about anything, really. I reach down to his other leg, and rip off a nice slab of prime Loudmouth. The dog releases its grip and starts to follow me. We get to the edge of the woods right by the road, and I throw the Loudmouth Lunch Special It lands in the middle of the road and the dog chases after it and begins his to enjoy his culinary delight. Loudmouth is upset about this, and begins to wail. I hold my stump up to his face to silence him, and Loudmouth's wailing becomes more muffled sobs. Steve and Charlie come up behind us, and we all watch the dog eating what used to be the back part of Loudmouth's good leg. We crouch low and wait for the truck. It gets closer to where we are, so I hobble back in the woods a little more, and everyone else follows.

The truck stops. The human can't run over a dog, and no matter how many times he honks his horn, that dog isn't moving. At all. Pretty humanitarian for someone delivering goods to a group of people who want to kill every zombie they meet. The human gets out of his truck in an attempt to either make the dog leave, or bring the dog along with him, and we make our move towards the back of the truck.

Mercifully enough, this delivery truck is low enough to the ground that we don't have to try and climb up too high. We get inside, the truck driver is none the wiser, and Loudmouth's dog growls at the driver and runs to the woods. Loudmouth begins his wailing again, but Steve and Charlie place their hands under his upper jaw and across his larynx, and the sounds go quiet quickly.

Our luck continues in the truck. There are a few shipping crates inside which provides us places to hide against. What we are going to do when they unload the truck, I have no idea. I don't even have an exit strategy here. I'm pretty focused on finding Anna if she's in here, and if she's still alive. I hear the gate open, and the truck lumbers through the gate.

I then hear the gate close behind us.

 Crap.

Even if we find Anna, how do we get out of here? I look to Steve for reassurance, and he responds with his usual gesture. I wish I had his confidence. Nothing seems to rattle Steve at all. The truck pulls up and comes to a halt. I can hear the driver talking to someone else outside. Whatever he is hauling in this load apparently is just dry goods, and there's no need to unload the truck until the next morning. Music to my ears. We lay in wait until nightfall before we even think about moving around this place.

We all slide out when it's been night for a while. We're trying to get a feel for the layout of this place, and I can hear Loudmouth's dog barking on the other side of the walls of wherever it is that we are currently at. There are houses here that look pretty nice, but it reminds me a lot of where I grew up. The humans here probably talk about each other the same way the people in my neighborhood did. We have to find Anna. I know she's in here somewhere. I just know it. We hear a golf cart coming down the street, so we take our place in the shadows. He drives by. Great. Security guards on golf carts is still a thing, apparently. With every step we take, I become more nervous. We creep past one house, and a cat hisses at us. Thank God that Loudmouth's dog is on the other side of the walls. It would give our position away for sure.

"Our position"?

Christ.

I sound exactly like one of those hunters. That's the last thing I need in my life. Charlie's rifle makes small thumps against his chest, but the noise level is nothing to be worried about I take attendance on all of us, and Loudmouth is missing. One guess where he is. We decide to leave him there and let him pet the cat as there will be considerably less noise if we leave him to his devices. We make our way down the street going between the houses in case Captain Cart decides to cruise on by with his crime stopping flashlight. There are a variety of what look to be trading stands littered down one road. One is labeled: "The Best Personal Defense Against the Zombie Horde! You've Tried the Rest, Now Try the BEST! Guaranteed to be Your First Line of Defense or Your Money Back to the Ones Who Survive You in Death!"

I thought that Loudmouth's slogan on his manager's name tag was dumb, but I think I may have found the grand champion of all dumb marketing ideas. Would you like to know what the best first line of defense against the zombie "horde" is? It's BEING A DECENT PERSON AND NOT TRYING TO KILL US EVERY FIFTEEN SECONDS. I don't think it's that hard, but apparently these people just don't get it at all. Case in point: right next to that clever little stand of puerile hatred is a box looking machine with a ridiculously over-sized mallet attached to it. My eyes are having trouble adjusting to make out what it is, but when they do, sure enough, it's a Whack-A-Zombie game for children. You're teaching your children to deal with something that is unfamiliar to them by placing a cartoon mallet in their hands and hit as many as they can in a certain time frame for cheap post-apocalyptic trinkets.

And somehow *zombies* are the real threat here?

I shake my head and we continue on. I don't know exactly what it is we're looking for. Anna could be in any one of these houses, or she could already be dead for all I know. As long as there is blood in what is left of my body, I'll do anything to stop that from happening. We come to the end of the road, and look right down another street. It seems to take us to that strip where I saw the trader stands and the charming game of skill for children. The street makes me nervous, but I also make out one of those signs that points people in multiple directions. Maybe that will give us a clue as to Anna's whereabouts. Miraculously enough, we make it to the sign undetected. Steve is staring at it like he can actually read it, but we all know that's not the truth. Charlie decides to keep watch by holding his gun and posting lookout. It would be a regal image, only Charlie's holding the barrel end of the gun where his trigger finger should be. If someone does come around, however, Charlie will be ready for whoever it is and will shake the butt of the rifle menacingly at him or her, I'm sure.

I read the sign, and all the words on the arrows make me want to power vomit. One direction is Lover's Lane, another direction is Forget Me Not Way, another one is Lost Until I Found You Drive (of course that one takes us down the main strip where all the trading stands are), and the last one is called Almost Paradise Court. That one not only draws my attention because I heard my parents play that song a million times when I was growing up, (and yes. They alternated the parts. Dad sang the male part, Mom sang the female part. Usually in very long car trips. Thank God for the evolution of mp3 players.) but also the sign below it which read: ZOMBIE RESPONSE CREW EDUCATION AND RECLAMATION CENTER.

That *has* to be where Anna is. They've kidnapped her to somehow brainwash her. These yokels must honestly believe that if they kidnap us, they can somehow educate us on how not to be a zombie. Like suddenly we take their three week correspondence course taught by Jennifer Sunshine and the other Stepford Wives of this quaint hamlet, our flesh will stop rotting and we'll be wearing the latest and greatest in high fashion. If we're not compliant with their wonderful teaching methods, well then I guess I know what all the guns are for. We're *zombies*, you dolt. No matter how you think your can change us, we are who we are. Period. We slink and hobble down that way as best we can. It take us a little longer for us to get to the front door, as the school is at the top of a small hill with a pretty steep embankment, but we get there. The front door of the facility is locked. Of course it is. Such a trusting society, but their doors are locked to outsiders. Everyone is welcome! Sure.

Steve peers through his shade at the lock, and pulls out his knife.

You have to be kidding me. This guy. Does he really think he can pick this lock with a knife? What in the world gives him this idea? Too many movies when he was human? I swear, I'm doomed. Nothing good can come of this half brained plan. I should have just stuck to looking for pizza and I wouldn't even be in this mess. Instead I get distracted by a woman who is running around with quite possibly three of the dumbest zombies I have ever met. Maybe that should have told me something. Maybe had I never been so distracted, I would be with my other zombies back in the woods. Maybe—

I hear a click, and the door opens.

I am so sorry, Steve. You may be the coolest and smartest zombie left on the planet.

We slowly push the door open. The light from the streetlamp allows a little bit of it to come in, but it's otherwise dark. I paw in the blindness searching for a switch. I find it, and suddenly the hallway is illuminated. It looks a lot like my old elementary school. There are cork bulletin boards on either side of the hallway announcing various accomplishments and displaying some of the "students'" work. Also, on either side of the hallway are different classrooms with the teachers' names on signs made of colorful construction paper. Their slogans are horrible too. "Miss Peeples' People". "Mr. Harrison's Humans". "Miss Richards' Rotting-Lesses". Can no one write a decent slogan anymore? Charlie gestures with the butt of his rifle for Steve and I to go on, and he will keep watch over the front door. We stroll slowly down the hall, and with every stumpy step I take, the sick feeling in my gut gets worse seeing all these horrible things on the wall They have been trying to teach them to write, and they have been displaying their "best work" on the walls outside. There are sheets of white paper with words that read "Im nauth a zumby enymoore. Im ah homan!" with the teacher's comments of "Great job!" at the bottom of it and an oblong smiley face drawn in green marker underneath. It's not that I'm against zombies knowing how to read and write, in fact Steve could use a few lessons. Just not from this nightmarish place.

Every fiber of my being is telling me not to look in to one of the classrooms, but out of morbid curiosity, I hobble up towards one of the classroom doors, open it slowly, and turn on the light. What I see is nothing short of criminal.

The entire room is painted in a brilliant sunshine shade of yellow, and there are generic looking children painted on the walls with round heads and that same goofy smile on all their faces. There are different activity stations set up around the room—art, math, reading—they even have a few beanbags set in the corner for the reading station. It looks like any elementary school classroom you have ever been in.
Until you look at the desks.

There are eight desks in this room, and there are eight zombies strapped down to each desk. There are straps that run across their backs and underneath the desks that force them to look as though they are just sleeping with their heads on their desks. I know for a fact that zombies don't sleep, so I motion for Steve to come with me to get a better look at them. No sooner than we get eye level with them, one breaks out in this panicked groan/scream hybrid. This makes the entire class break out into the same sound. They're being tortured. They don't even recognize us as fellow zombies. I can see the fear and panic in their faces. We have to do something to help them, and I know it. The problem is that in their feral condition, I'm not sure that they wouldn't turn on us. I put my stump on one of the desks, and notice that the desk itself is shaky. Makes sense—no one I know wants to be in a desk for long, and being strapped face down to one isn't exactly a day at the local county fair. The zombies have been shaking these desks to where they are pretty flimsy. I look at Steve, not knowing what we should do. Steve has an expression on his face that he has no clue as well. I decide to go to the front of the building and get Charlie. I bring him into the classroom, and he is furiously shaking the rifle butt of his gun at a poster that has a drawing of a zombie evolving into a "real man".

I don't know what the reaction is all about, but our mild-mannered Charlie has snapped. He immediately grabs one of the desks and starts dragging it out into the hallway. Steve and I follow Charlie out to try and figure out what he's up to. The zombie strapped to the desk starts to shake as hard as it can, and Charlie keeps dragging it towards the front door. He drags it outside, and there is an incredibly loud crash that happens next. The feral zombie is on the ground at the bottom of the embankment, but his straps have come loose. He's free.

Is this a *good* thing?
Charlie looks back at us and points back to the classroom. Alright. Operation: ZombieLiberation has commenced. Steve and I head back to the room, and Charlie follows. We empty out as many classrooms as we can, (and thankfully, it's a small building) and drag the ferals to their freedom at the bottom of the hill. Desks crash repeatedly, and it draws the attention of Captain Cart who shines the light of truth and justice when he arrives on the scene. I can see the fear in his face from where I'm standing. He shines the light up to us, and I give him the biggest stump salute of his life. He pulls out a radio to call for backup, but by that time, the ferals are making their way down the main street and are destroying every trading stand the humans have here. I hope you're ready to rumble, Zombie Response Crew.

I didn't find Anna anywhere in all of those classrooms, so I head to what looks like an administrator's office. Maybe there's something about her in there. At this point, I'll take anything.. The door opens, and I dread that it does. I always hated whenever I would be called up to it. Not that I was a bad kid—I wasn't. It's just that I always got called up for things that really didn't have anything to do with me.

There was this time in first grade when I had a box of crayons that had these new colors and Teddy Chance told me that he would give me three pieces of candy if I would let him borrow some of the newer colors because he was working on this really awesome dragon and he wanted to finish the masterpiece before recess. Idiot that I was, I immediately accepted the deal. Three pieces of candy as payment for renting my crayons? Chance, you foolish mortal. I'll take that any day, sucker.

What I failed to realize is the three pieces of candy Teddy offered me were ones that he had stolen from the teacher's desk. As I packed all three pieces into my mouth, the teacher walked over to my desk and asked me what I just ate. I only responded by gazing back at her with a cheek full of ill-gotten gains. I was sent to the principal's office where I had to listen to him call my mom while Teddy finished his artwork with my periwinkle crayon.
I rifle through the desk looking for something. I don't know what, but anything that would help me find Anna would work for me. I find a folder inside the desk that is labeled "unteachable" and underneath it a label that reads "ship west". I open it up and begin furiously scanning the documents inside. One talks about a female that just stares out the window of the classroom all day like she's looking for something. Non-violent, no altercations with staff, but unwilling to learn any of the lessons that have been taught. Just stares out the window. No interactions with other zombies, constantly trying to get her hair out of her face.

Anna.

She's been shipped west.

It's time to bounce. Time to get out of here, immediately. I go back to the front of the building, and Charlie and Steve are checking out the chaos that is unfolding. The humans are trying to shoot as many of the ferals that they can, and the ferals are running around trashing as much of the place that they can. My eye is drawn to one in particular that has dislodged the mallet from the game and is chasing one of the citizens around and hitting him in the back of the head with it. We try to make our way back to where Loudmouth is in the midst of this panic and confusion with minimal human contact as much as possible. Unfortunately, that's not the way it works. A hunter spots us and raises his gun, ordering Charlie to drop his rifle. Charlie isn't having it. The hunter gives the order again. I'm standing next to Charlie, and I have my hand and stump up in the air. I'm surrendering, but Charlie isn't. The hunter orders Charlie to lower his weapon again. Steve has also joined me in putting his hands in the air. Chill out, Charlie. Lower the rifle, man. Charlie raises the butt of the rifle towards the hunter, and I notice that the hunter's gun is shaking. I don't think he really wants to kill us at all. He's just been so brainwashed that he doesn't know any better. *Something* is making him shake. Charlie's groans get louder— aggressive as he shakes the butt of the rifle towards the hunter. A gunshot goes off. It's very close to me, and it's very loud. My hand and stump drops, and I'm feeling all over my body for any wounds. It's an experiment in futility. All my body is covered in wounds of some sort that have never healed, so how would I notice any new ones? My head turns towards Charlie, who I find is no longer standing next to me. The hunter has the same look of confusion on his face as did the one who we tied to the tree with jumper cables. I look behind me and Charlie is lying motionless on the ground. The hunter is frozen in his stance. I can't process what just happened. Not Charlie. Charlie was my friend. Yes, he was a little too obsessed with cleaning up after the outbreak, but that's where he was at his happiest. And you killed him because of some brainwashed cult's teachings? *All* zombies are feral? *We're* the enemy? Get ready to see feral, hunter. You're about to see it like you never have in your life. Or the last few seconds of it anyway.

I stand up and rush at the hunter, giving him my best impression of a feral. More to the point, I take one really quick step towards him with the fiercest grunt I can muster, and fall flat on my face. I didn't take the time to get my balance right, and my leg stump didn't want to cooperate with my initial course of action.

Now one of my friends is dead, the love of my life is somewhere out west, no one seems to have any pizza whatsoever, and I am inhaling a lovely patch of unpaved road. If you're looking for a hero, keep looking. I'm sure he or she is somewhere out there, but clearly I am not it.

 Steve follows my lead and charges towards the hunter. He must be new because he turns and runs towards the gate. Maybe he was out of bullets. You know, using that last one in his gun to kill one of my friends. I make my way towards Steve and we grin through our tears at watching society's salvation run like a little girl who is excited about her new bike at Christmas.

Charlie would have loved this scene. If noting else, he would have loved the ability to clean up after all this mess calmed down. I lean my stump on Steve's back, and he leans his hand on my shoulder. I then discover that the hand on my shoulder is attached. To Charlie.

There was a gunshot, yes. Charlie found the trigger, and shot himself in the shoulder thinking he was pointing the barrel at the hunter. I'm not a fan of hunters, but Charlie hates them so much that he would shoot himself in the shoulder. We make our way back to Loudmouth, and he is still petting that cat in the midst of all this insanity. More to the point, he must have been feeding the cat some strips of his face, as the cat is now permanently affixed to his shoulder and is licking and chewing on the open sores where Loudmouth's cheek used to be. Loudmouth's eyes are squinting, so I know he's grinning at us. More than likely, he's also laughing about seeing the gaping hole in Charlie's shoulder. The gates are open—the hunters must have figured that they weren't prepared when their ideas to re-educate zombies went horribly awry, and in their fleeing panic no one stuck around to close the gate. We make our way out avoiding the ferals. We go out to the road, and Loudmouth's dog sprints towards his spot on his leg. Cat on the shoulder, dog on the leg. Loudmouth the animal lover, ladies and gentlemen. We make our way back to the woods as the sun begins to shine.

9.

IT HAS been an interesting few weeks, no doubt. Not that time really means anything when you're a zombie, but when you have so many things occur that are out of your normal routine of wandering aimlessly and looking for pizza in a world where it may not exist, interesting is the best term I can think of to describe all the events that have happened in a relatively short amount of time.
Meet new friends? Check. Find love of my life? Check. Have love of my life kidnapped by a lunatic cult who obviously believes that being a zombie is just a phase we're going through? Check.

What's even more strange is that I see these guys as my family. We have been through enough in the past weeks that it sort of makes sense to me. When I was a human, I was too weird to really belong anywhere, and I think my family just sort of tolerated who I was without actually sitting down and talking to me like I was a regular human. I'm not judged by these guys, and I never was judged by Anna. I guess it's true that you don't have to be blood to be family.

As we wander through the woods, I know this is just the beginning of the story. I don't know where it will lead us. I don't know if all of us will make it out west. I don't know if that cat and that dog will stay permanently stuck to Loudmouth's face and leg. I don't know much of anything, but the one thing that I can add to my list of certainties is that for once in my life, I have a family. I have a sense of belonging. I don't have pizza, but that will hopefully be rectified as we go on this journey. All of us together. Living, laughing, rotting—if there was a four-seater bike, we would all be on it.

Granted, I would have a problem with pedaling and hanging on, but with our belief in each other, we could make it work. I just know it. I look over to Steve, and he's flashing the bony thumbs up. I look behind me, and Loudmouth is still grinning and now pointing at Charlie's open wound on his shoulder while the cat and dog feast away on his face and his leg.

This is my family now. I used to think that it was all about me and my quest for pizza, but now I realize that this is a story of all of us. The fall breeze blows gently through my open sores, and for once, I look up at the partial canopy of the forest and realize that even if things don't turn out for the four of us on this trip, it's cool. We found each other. That's what really matters in life. To make this circle complete, however, I have to find Anna. That's why we're going to head west. It shouldn't be that difficult. The sun sets in the west, so we'll just head away from where it's rising.

My thoughts wander to how great the fall breeze feels on my wounds. There's that cooler tinge to the air today, and it smells nice through my exposed nasal cavities The fallen leaves crunch underneath my stump, and just feeling them on the infected wound makes it feel slightly better. Maybe Frankie Shack's parents were on to something with this whole embracing nature thing. While it might feel good on my stump, it still doesn't belong on pizza. That's just unacceptable. Fix your life.

Lost in my own thoughts, I stumble and fall down. Now I'm just breathing in leaves and the appetizing allure of anaerobic decay. Awesome. So much for my moment of reflection. Everyone comes to help me back up, and we start back on our path. Incredibly slow, but on our path nonetheless.

I don't care how long it takes. I'm going to find her. I'm going to be with her. We're going to be together and live the rest of our decaying lives like any other boy and girl zombie would.

And if I'm incredibly fortunate, I might find some pizza. That would be completely awesome.

About the Author

Jason Appling has taught high school English for nineteen years. He lives with his wife and a small farm of dogs and cats outside of Atlanta, Georgia. He has an unhealthy obsession with the band Motorhead, Funko Pops, bad horror movies, and worse kung fu movies. This is his first book. Be kind.

A Zombie. A Purpose. A Quest. Before you roll your eyes, gentle reader, know that the actions of this book take place through the eyes of the zombie himself. Witness now the first part of a four part series that focuses on Edgar and his adventures of merry (yet rotting) zombies as they make their way through an uncaring post-outbreak society in which--

Actually, he just wants pizza. Things happen. You should probably read what's inside the book instead of the back cover. Look at you. Judging a book by its cover. Shame, shame.

Jason Appling has taught high school English for 19 years, and he lives with his beautiful wife and their small farm of dogs and cats an hour outside of Atlanta, Georgia. He has an unhealthy obsession with Motorhead, Funko Pops, and bad horror movies.

ISBN 9781521793688

9 781521 793688

In a mountain bike, look for a relaxed geometric design that gives comfort and stability of ride, 1-3/4-inch to 2-1/2-inch wide tires that will give good traction and shock absorption, a wide gear selection for use in a variety of terrain, and cantilever brakes.

There are excellent, good, and not-so-good mountain bikes on the market. Consider frame materials, components, durability, weight, and serviceability when purchasing a mountain bike.

Remember the differences between mountain bikes and city or hybrid bikes. City bikes resemble mountain bikes in appearance but are not as strong and usually have narrower, less knobby tires and fewer gears. City and hybrid bikes begin at a lower price than do mountain bikes. If all of your riding will be on relatively flat pavement, and budget is a primary concern, a hybrid or city bike may be your best choice. If you plan to ride a variety of terrain, spend more for a mountain bike. You won't regret it.

As one of the world's fastest-growing sports and fitness activities, mountain biking is changing rapidly. There is much innovation. We've already seen the introduction (but not refinement) of the all-wheel-drive mountain bike. Other designers are working on collapsible mountain bikes that can be packed in a suitcase. New technology is making today's midpriced mountain bikes far superior to the top-of-the-line models of just a few years ago. Although today's mountain bike has opened a whole new world of adventure, there is no doubt we are still in the sport's infancy.

Take a Ride!

With the newfound freedom of this sturdy piece of equipment, you'll be able to escape the hurried rush of motor vehicles on the pavement of your community. You will become an authority on what lies at the end of each dirt road in the area. (One reminder: Good mountain bikers never trespass on private property.) You will reach new heights of mental and physical well-being, and you will experience fun and adventure as never before.

Is this your idea of outdoor enjoyment? Stop in at your local bicycle shop. Take a test ride. This is where the adventure begins.

David Epperson

Exploring off-road at Lake Catamount, Colorado.

The bicycle dates to the late 1700s and has clearly come a long way in its 200-year history. The mountain bike has been around only since the late 1970s and early 1980s. In its own way, it has come just as far.

Tom Ritchey, Gary Fisher, Charles Kelly, and others in Marin County, California, are generally credited with developing the mountain bike, starting out by gathering old bikes and using the parts to fashion a basic five-speed clunker.

Until this time, cycling's focus had been on youth bikes and the 10-speed, or road bike. But in the early 1980s, the mountain bike began to make rapid inroads into bicycle sales.

The wave of mountain biking spread from initial hotbeds in northern California and Colorado across the United States to Canada, Europe, Australia, New Zealand, and the Far East.

Within one short decade, the mountain bike became firmly established as the basic bicycle of adult Americans and accounted for a majority of the 11.6 million bicycles sold in the country. That's quite a jump from the total 1 million bicycles made in the United States during the so-called Bicycle Age year of 1899! This is indeed the Age of the Mountain Bike.

Mountain Bike Growth

According to the Bicycle Institute of America, more than 20 million Americans ride mountain bikes today, up from just 200,000 in 1983 and 2.6 million in 1986.

Just how much of the bicycle market the mountain bike will eventually capture is anybody's guess. In many small mountain towns and resort areas, mountain bikes already account for 90 percent or more of all full-size bicycle sales. Industry experts estimate that mountain bikes presently account for about two thirds of all full-size bicycle sales.

All the major bicycle manufacturers that have made road bikes, plus many others, are now making mountain bikes. There are about 20 major mountain bike manufacturers and literally hundreds of "garage companies" making custom, hand-built frames.

Membership in the National Off-Road Bicycle Association (NORBA), the U.S. mountain bike race sanctioning organization founded in 1983, demonstrates the sport's increasing popularity. In 1992, the group neared the 20,000 mark in membership and was asked to sanction about 500 races, up from 100 in just three years.

While most mountain bike competitors are 17 to 26 years old, NORBA officials point out that there are so many different kinds of people riding mountain bikes today it would be impossible to develop a profile of a typical mountain bike rider.

There's no one typical profile of a mountain biker.

The International Mountain Biking Association (IMBA) is perhaps the most representative group for mountain biking on an international level. It is dedicated to educating people on mountain biking as an environmentally sound and sustainable activity.

Based in Los Angeles, IMBA is affiliated with clubs across the United States, Canada, Italy, Finland, Spain, and Puerto Rico. IMBA receives industry support in North America, Europe, and Japan.

RIDING THE RUBICON TRAIL

This high country adventure had been in the back of my mind for years. A new invention called the mountain bike finally made it possible. On an August day in 1980, I rode a mountain bike across California's Sierra Nevada mountains, on the famed Rubicon Trail near Lake Tahoe.

Conditions were ideal. The pine-scented air, crystal-clear blue sky, and towering mountain peaks filled me with anticipation and a profound appreciation for the great outdoors. Early morning temperatures were mild, but would be warm before long.

A friend had driven me from my South Lake Tahoe home into the mountains, across Echo Summit, to my predetermined starting point, the tiny community of Riverton on Highway 50. We reviewed my route and the approximate time I hoped to return.

Saying good-bye, I gave my bike a final safety check and took a quick inventory of my essentials for the day. Everything seemed to be in order—helmet, spare tube, patch kit, tools, first-aid kit, sunscreen, and, of course, a topographic map with my route highlighted.

I was ready to ride, to begin the 60-mile (97-km) 1-day journey that is perhaps the most memorable ride I have taken in 30 years of bicycling.

The inspiration for this ride began abstractly about 10 years earlier. I was working at a lodge at Lake Tahoe and met a family who had just finished a 2-day jeep ride on what they described as the most beautiful four-wheel-drive road in the Sierra Nevada.

They had crossed the Rubicon Trail, a rugged and historic mountain crossing that over the years has become known for its annual jeep trek and as the ultimate proving ground for off-road vehicles.

At the time, I was a competitive cyclist, very much into training 60 to 120 miles (97 to 194 km) each day on my sleek road bike. Although the idea of the mountain bike never occurred to me, I remember being fascinated by the idea of cycling on rough mountain roads.

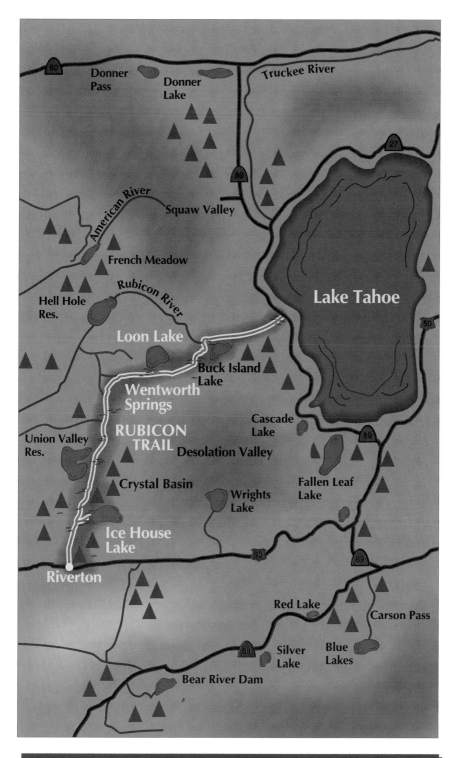

Donner Pass

Donner Lake

Truckee River

Lake Tahoe

American River

Squaw Valley

French Meadow

Rubicon River

Hell Hole Res.

Loon Lake

Buck Island Lake

Wentworth Springs

RUBICON TRAIL

Cascade Lake

Union Valley Res.

Desolation Valley

Crystal Basin

Wrights Lake

Fallen Leaf Lake

Ice House Lake

Riverton

Red Lake

Carson Pass

Silver Lake

Blue Lakes

Bear River Dam

So there I was 10 years later, ready to pedal off into a long-fantasized journey. With me was my first mountain bike, one of the first in the region, and I knew I had found the perfect place to try it out. As I climbed onto the saddle, I thought about the potential of this brand-new form of bicycling—the freedom, the outdoors, the excitement. To me, there was no doubt that this was bicycling's future.

I pedaled slowly as I warmed up along a deserted 20-mile (32-km) stretch of pavement that swept gently toward the towering Sierra crest. The warm sun and gorgeous terrain filled my senses. My first destination was Ice House Lake, the first of numerous lakes on my route.

Soon the shimmering waters of Ice House appeared as my first reward. I rode onward to Wentworth Springs and Loon Lake. Here the pavement ended and the mountain bike challenge of the Rubicon Trail began.

By about 11 a.m. I had pedaled 25 miles (40 km) along a beautiful country road. My first challenge was to locate the Rubicon trailhead. The map showed where the route began but the trail was not readily apparent. After carefully scanning the area, I decided this ride might be tougher than I had imagined.

I pushed and carried my bike up a steep ravine, which appeared to be the only probable route. Traces of black tire tracks and tiny oil stains on a few rocks were my only clues that vehicles had traveled this rugged path. When I finally emerged onto the ridge, I saw more of what appeared to be a trail. The area was very rough and during the first few miles, only chipped rock and tire traces on the granite slabs kept me on track.

As I reveled in this top-of-the-world wilderness, I still wasn't sure I was, in fact, on the Rubicon Trail. I hadn't seen a soul. I studied my map and rode on. I came upon small lakes that seemed to confirm I was on course. As I traveled on, the day warmed. I took breaks and swam in clear alpine lakes, enjoying their freshness and the solitude of high mountain meadows.

Finally, I saw a vehicle slowly moving toward me. I wondered how anyone could negotiate a vehicle across this steep route. The people in the vehicle were perhaps more amazed at how a bicycle could cross such terrain. At this time, most people had yet to see a mountain bike.

The jeepsters confirmed we were on the Rubicon Trail but suggested it would take me hours to ride the remaining 10 miles (16 km) to the shores of Lake Tahoe. It was 1 p.m. and I figured I could cover 10 miles by dark, even if I had to walk all the way. Even so, I curtailed the leisurely stops for swims and relaxation.

I pedaled with a renewed confidence. I actually caught and passed a few vehicles picking their way over the bumpy trail. I realized a bicycle could cover this terrain more gracefully than a motorized vehicle.

I rode harder, became more determined in my pace, and focused on the terrain with renewed intensity. The Rubicon was an ideal testing ground for a mountain bike; it tested all of my riding skills. Giant slabs of granite made some sections simple and fun. But then the trail would drop into ravines for true tests of riding ability.

Rocks of every shape and size cover the trail. Picking the right line and pedaling smoothly over obstacles is mountain biking at its best. Stream crossings abound as the Rubicon weaves its way over the mountains, and over every rise the view is spectacular. These are the reasons I have returned to this trail several times, bringing friends to share an unmatched experience.

After 16 miles (26 km) along the heart of the Rubicon, I crested the final ridge and could see the blue expanse of Lake Tahoe below me. I paused and felt satisfaction in my experiences of the day. Again I realized the magic in mountain biking.

By 6 p.m. I had not only descended to civilization along Lake Tahoe's shore, but also pedaled home to South Lake Tahoe, 20 paved miles (32 km) beyond the trailhead. I checked in with my friend, and as we talked about the ride, I began to realize this was only the beginning of my mountain bike discovery.

I thought about exploring endless trails, how mountain biking can open new opportunities for hikers and other outdoor enthusiasts, how it can bring year-round enjoyment and training to winter sports enthusiasts, how people of all ages would someday discover the mountain bike.

—Don Davis

Where to Find the Right Bike

A comfortable bike of the correct size should be the first concern for the potential mountain biker. As with any other major purchase of specialized equipment, it pays to study up and shop around. Ask for recommendations from cycling friends and acquaintances, check out the cycling magazines, and watch for ads in your local newspapers.

Shopping for a Bike Shop

Where you buy your mountain bike is just as important as what kind of bike you buy, maybe even more so. When you begin to look for a mountain bike, you should first choose a bike shop, and consider several aspects.

In riding a bicycle, as in driving a car, you need access to professional advice, a good supply of parts, and a top-flight mechanic. This means the shop where you purchase your bike—and the shop where you will probably have it serviced—should be as close as possible to where you live or work. If you travel long distances to save a few dollars on a bicycle, will you be willing to travel again for parts, minor tune-ups, or adjustments?

Shop mechanics often hesitate to work on bikes bought elsewhere; they will advise you to visit the shop where you bought your bicycle. Of course, most mechanics are understandably reluctant to work on brands they are not familiar with.

As a consumer, you should feel confident your bike shop has knowledgeable sales and service personnel. Is it a full-service shop? Can it handle all your service needs, from fitting you properly at the original sale to possibly building a new wheel or aligning a damaged frame? Does the shop handle a wide range of bikes so you and your family can be satisfied now and in the future if you choose to upgrade?

Your shop should be able to satisfy all your equipment needs including good and timely service and parts ordering. If a part is not in stock, the shop should gladly special order it for you.

Buying at a nearby shop will make it easier for you to get your bike's 30-day after-purchase service as well as any subsequent tune-ups. The postpurchase service is provided free by reputable bike shops for nearly all major brands of bicycles and is perhaps the most important visit you will make to your bike shop after the original purchase.

A good shop's salespeople will listen to your needs and make appropriate recommendations. If the salesperson isn't interested in listening

It's a good idea to buy your mountain bike from the shop where you expect to have it serviced.

and insists on telling you what to buy, consider it a warning to visit another bike shop. Sure, it's wise to take advantage of the salesperson's experience, but it should be on your terms.

CONSUMER TIP

Some shops may offer a 1-year or lifetime warranty on new mountain bikes. These are offered either as part of the purchase or as an extra-cost extended service contract. While good shops will back up this promise, others may use it only to attract your initial investment.

Long warranties have been used as a sales gimmick, causing the consumer to pay too much for the bike. The shop may be betting the buyer will forget or otherwise pass up the opportunity for extended service.

In any case, read the fine print on any shop warranties. Does the warranty cover wear and tear caused by regular use? Does it cover labor and parts? Find out what exactly it provides.

Test Rides and Rentals

There is no better way to select a bicycle than by taking a test ride. It's no different from selecting a new vehicle. Most bike shops will be happy to let you take a spin around the neighborhood, but be aware that in most cases you won't be able to take off-road test rides.

Many shops have demo models that you can rent and test off-road. And many of these shops will apply the rental charge to your eventual purchase price.

Mountain bike magazines (see appendix) feature regular reviews of various models of bikes. These provide lots of good information, but don't put all your faith in the reviews. Bike riders, like movie critics, have different preferences, and many of the reviews are geared to the more advanced rider.

One of the best ways to get a feel for differences in the many mountain bike models is to ride at one of the many ski resorts that have summertime mountain bike programs. They have good quality rental and demo bikes, usually in varying brands, models, and sizes. You may be able to attend

You can test-ride various mountain bikes on off-road conditions at a rental facility like this one.

a demo day where numerous brands and models will be available for test riding. Obviously, being able to compare different bikes on the same day in identical riding conditions can be of great help.

How to Choose a Mountain Bike

Before you go bike shopping, carefully consider your needs. Believe it or not, you can spend several thousand dollars for a fully equipped, top-of-the-line competition bike. Few of us need or can afford this kind of equipment. You should decide on a price range based on how often and where you plan to ride. This is important information. Your bike salesperson will ask these questions and then suggest options based on your plans and budget.

As in buying most specialized equipment, personal preference plays a major role in bicycle selection. Test-ride everything you can. Look for durability, light weight, index shifting, powerful brakes, and good ground clearance.

Underbuying is one of the most common mistakes made by the first-time bike buyer. You'll see an advertised special and buy the bike, perhaps from a large discount chain outlet, only to discover later that you need more than this heavy, entry-level clunker offers. Don't cut yourself short.

Price Ranges

How much should you pay for a mountain bike? If you try buying a cheap bike, you risk reduced satisfaction and increased chance of breakdown.

If you plan to stay on the pavement, you should be able to find a suitable hybrid or city bike for less than $300. Remember, the less-beefy city bikes won't handle tough off-road terrain.

If you plan some serious off-road riding, you should consider the $350 to $450 price range. This will buy a bike with a sturdy chro-moly steel frame and components that will stand up to most of the rigors of off-road riding.

In the $450 to $550 price range, you will step up to a more advanced frame geometry, perhaps other frame materials, and better components. You'll have a bike that shifts easier, brakes better, and perhaps has shock absorption. Your off-road experience will be more comfortable.

Moving into the advanced lines, from about $750 into the thousands of dollars, you will reach peak levels in high-tech function and durability. You will enjoy the exotic lightweight materials and top-of-the-line components used by the sport's top competitors.

■ FIND YOUR PRICE RANGE

Write next to each number below the letter that corresponds to how you'd most likely answer each of the following questions. When you're finished, score 1 point for every *a* answer, 2 for every *b*, and 3 for every *c*. Check the scoring key at the end of the questionnaire to find out the price range you should start looking in to find the kind of bike that will best fit your riding needs. Price ranges are in U.S. dollars.

1. How sure are you that mountain biking will become a regular part of your activity schedule?
   a. Not very. I just want to try the activity.
   b. Pretty sure.
   c. Very sure.
2. Where do you intend to ride?
   a. Mostly on-road.
   b. About the same on-road and off-road.
   c. Mostly off-road.
3. How many miles (kilometers) off-road do you think you'll ride each week?
   a. Under 15 miles (25 km).
   b. Fifteen to 30 miles (25-50 km).
   c. Over 30 miles (50 km).

Key

0-3 points, start looking in the $200 to $400 range
4-6 points, start looking in the $400 to $800 range
7-9 points, start looking in the $800 and up range

Bike Size and Reach

Buying the right size bike is the foremost consideration. Frame sizes start at about 16 inches (40.6 cm) for youths and range upward to about 23 inches (58.4 cm). Most adults use 20- or 21-inch (50.8- or 53.3-cm) mountain bikes with 26-inch wheels. Kid's sizes range from 16-inch (40.6-cm) frames with 20-inch wheels to 18-inch (45.7-cm) or so frames with 24-inch wheels.

Frame size is traditionally measured from the top of the seat tube to the center of the bottom bracket spindle.

A mountain bike is fitted to the rider in much the same way any other bike is fitted. But because you will be riding on bumpy, uneven terrain, you should have more clearance at the top tube. For mountain bikes, when you stand and straddle the top tube, you should have 2 to 4 inches (5 to 10 cm) of clearance between your crotch and the frame. If you plan to ride in very rough terrain, you may want added clearance for safety reasons.

Reach from seat to handlebar is a key factor in sizing and an important consideration for your riding comfort, as well as your ability to pedal with power. Generally your seat should be positioned about 2 inches (5 cm) higher than your handlebar. This allows for a dynamic body position with more power, better weight distribution, and proper leverage when climbing.

A bike that is too big can take you for a ride—it can be dangerous and difficult to handle and could possibly lead to a serious accident. Conversely, a bike that is too small will give you a cramped feeling, and you won't be comfortable or efficient in your riding.

If you are uncertain in your knowledge of bike size, frame material, the bike's working condition, or price, shop with someone who is more familiar with mountain biking. They can help you determine value and give you a better chance of scoring a great deal.

Opportunities for finding good, previously owned mountain bikes are getting better all the time. Riders are moving up to higher quality models and young people are moving up to larger frames, creating a pool of used mountain bikes for people of all ages.

Used mountain bikes are found in bicycle shops, through ads on bike shop or school or college bulletin boards, and through local classified ads. Some of the more populated regions have shops or publications specializing in used cycles and cycling and sports equipment.

There are great buys to be found if you know what you are looking for. Compare prices and features with new models on the market. You can expect a good mountain bike to depreciate in value by 10 percent to 20 percent per year and then level out in the $200 to $400 range.

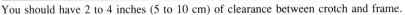

You should have 2 to 4 inches (5 to 10 cm) of clearance between crotch and frame.

Frames

Today's mountain bike frames are made of many different materials, some very sophisticated and each with its own advantages. Steel remains the industry standard frame material.

High-tensile or high-carbon steels are generally heavier and not as strong as chrome-molybdenum (chro-moly). These types of steel are usually found in the most inexpensive mountain bikes and should be avoided if you plan to leave the pavement.

Most steel-frame mountain bikes are TIG (tungsten inert gas) welded. This type of welding can be recognized by the rough appearance of the weld at a joint. The other way of joining tubes or adding fittings is brazing. This is usually done with silver or brass. A lug is usually used to attach tubes with the brazing process.

Steel-frame bikes are the most popular because of their cost, durability, comfort, and service life.

You will find other materials in mountain bike frames including aluminum, carbon fiber, and titanium.

But, the first-time buyer will probably be happiest with a double-butted chro-moly frame. Always keep in mind that proper design, fit, assembly, and adjustment are much more important than frame materials in the bike's overall feel and performance.

AT A GLANCE: FRAME MATERIALS

	Advantages	*Disadvantages*	*Dollar range*
Chro-moly steel	Strength and stiffness Ease of repair Low price	Weight Rougher ride	$200-$1,500
Aluminum	Light weight Smooth ride Responsiveness	Greater variation in ride qualities Difficulty of repair	$600-$3,000
Carbon fiber	Light weight Smooth ride Responsiveness	Fragility to certain impacts Cost of repair	$800-$3,000
Titanium	Strength Responsiveness Durability	High cost	$2,000 and up

Component Choices

Bicycle components, primarily shifters and derailleurs and brake levers and brakes, are a chief factor in bicycle pricing. Ask your bike shop about the differences in components from various manufacturers. A select few large component makers dominate the field internationally. Each makes several lines or groups of components.

Gears and Brakes

Check the feel of various shifters and brake levers, which vary in size, shape, and speed of function. Do you prefer the motorcycle feel of a grip shifter to the standard thumb shifter? Ask about features such as Shimano's

Frame Materials

Chro-moly Steel

If you plan to ride off-road, your steel frame should be chro-moly (cr-mo) steel throughout, including frame and forks and it should be double-butted. If you hear the terms triple-butted or quad-butted, these are even stronger. Butting is the process that makes the tube walls thicker at the ends than in the middle, giving the greatest strength at the joints. The tubes taper off to a thinner wall in the middle, saving weight. Triple- or quad-butted frames have three or four different thicknesses within the tube, rather than just two.

David Epperson

David Epperson

Aluminum Tubing

Weight is the greatest advantage of aluminum; it is three times lighter than steel. It is weaker and more flexible, depending on diameter and tube wall thickness. Thus, when you look at aluminum bikes you will often see over-sized tubing for greater strength. After matching the strength of steel in an aluminum bike you will usually wind up with a frame weight savings of 10 percent to 20 percent. The aluminum frame will save weight, and it can provide a stiffer or softer ride, depending on tubing size and design goals of the manufacturer.

Carbon Fiber

These are composite man-made materials of glass carbon, polyester, or carbon. The fibers are glued, usually with epoxy, and layered for strength. Carbon fiber frames are molded to achieve proper strength and ridability. This material holds great promise but is expensive. Carbon fiber does save some weight but has yet to prove durable enough for rugged mountain bike use.

David Epperson

Titanium Tubing

Glamorous and expensive, it doesn't rust and doesn't need paint. Used in satellites and aircraft, titanium is the most exotic material used in mountain bike construction. It weighs 40 percent less than steel and is reported to be as strong as any chro-moly. Titanium comes closest to matching steel in all respects and is better in durability and service life. However, titanium is very expensive and will probably stay that way in the near future.

David Epperson

Hyperglide which smooths your shifting. Remember that there is a huge aftermarket and these and other components can be changed later if you like.

Suspension

The mountain bike rage of the '90s has been suspension, a feature now offered by nearly every mountain bike manufacturer. Most companies use shock absorbing suspension forks in the front, some offer rear suspension, and others have come up with various futuristic designs. Initial concerns about increased weight versus performance have been alleviated by the introduction of new front shocks that add very little to total bike weight.

Shock absorbers need to react at high and low speeds; therefore, adjustable models may be better. Look for shocks with easy access for on-the-trail adjustment. Suspension is most cost-effective when purchased on a new bike; retrofitting remains expensive, although costs are coming down.

Nearly every mountain bike racer is now using suspension but not all riders agree it is necessary. Test-ride a suspension-equipped bike and decide for yourself.

Front shocks.

Handlebars

Width is a consideration. You want your hands to be spread comfortably. Bar ends can be attached to the handlebars to create an alternative hand position.

DO YOU NEED SHOCK ABSORBERS?

I ride an Allsop bike, which has been one of the more unusual looking bikes on the market in recent years. The Allsop Softride Suspension System is different from most suspension systems. It suspends the rider rather than the bike.

Other systems use shock absorbers on the front forks and maybe in the stem and rear, but the Allsop system places the saddle on a resin-molded carbon fiber suspension beam that is attached in front to the frame. It also features a shock-absorbing stem. It's unique and may look odd, but I find that it provides high levels of comfort and performance.

Suspension in mountain bikes is at the stage of innovation and debate. Manufacturers have been taking cues from the motorcycle industry in developing their suspension technologies.

Although many bikes come stock with suspension, the concept still has a long way to go. The first-time buyer should consider components and frame first and not place too much emphasis on suspension.

—Don Davis

Stem

This part attaches your handlebar to the headset. Look for a lightweight stem with a shape that gives you a comfortable position and reach from seat to handlebar. Shock absorbing stems are also available.

Crankset

Your cranks attach your pedals to the crankset. Large, round chainrings provide smooth spinning. Many bikes are equipped with out-of-round inner rings for power pedaling.

Pedals

New riders may stick with the standard bicycle pedal, but in rough terrain a standard pedal may allow the foot to slip, causing a lower body collision with the top tube. You may want to add toe clips. Once you get the hang of flipping into your clips, you'll wonder how you rode without them. Many advanced riders use clipless pedals that, when used with compatible cycling shoes, offer precise control through step-in entry and quick release, like a ski binding.

Wheels, Spokes

Mountain bike wheels and spokes are designed for heavy-duty use. You shouldn't have to worry about wobbly or dinged wheels.

Tires

Bicycle tires have different tread designs with the knobby, high-traction mountain bike tire at one end of spectrum and the skinny, high-speed road tire at the other. Look for wide lugs on the side of the tread to help in cornering at speed and for mud release. Most riders use identical front and rear tires but some will use a front tire designed for more steering control. Some tire makers offer specially designed front and rear tires. There are cross tires designed for both road and off-road riding.

Saddle

Your mount won't give you a lot of pleasure if it isn't saddled with a comfortable seat. Look first at the saddle size, shape, and width. Compare it to your size, shape, and width. Anatomy comes first. If standard padding doesn't cut it, there are several fine, self-molding saddles on the market. Gel-like substances, flow liquids, and fluids are designed into saddles. The idea is to equalize pressure, reduce pressure points, and provide a softer cushion.

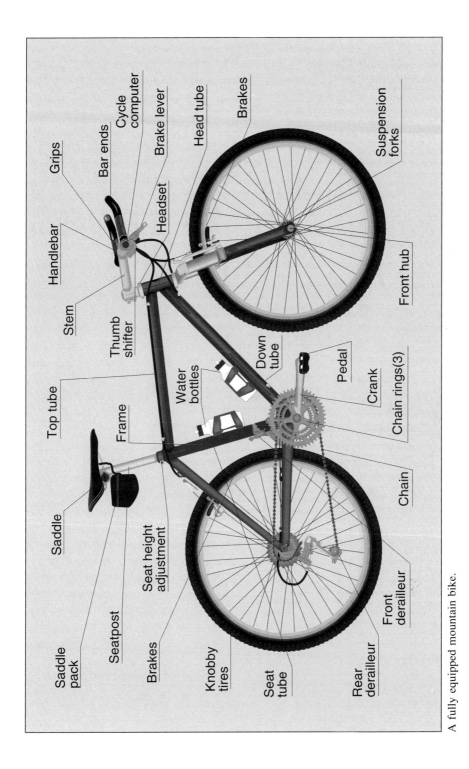

A fully equipped mountain bike.

Getting the Right Safety Gear, Apparel, and Accessories

To ride comfortably and successfully, a mountain biker needs more than just a well-equipped bike. Safety gear is essential, and the right clothing and accessories make riding more enjoyable.

Suiting Up for Safety

You need to make sure you have the necessary gear to ride safely. Protecting yourself from injuries as a result of spills or from the effects of the sun will allow you to concentrate on enjoying your ride.

Helmets

The helmet is unquestionably the mountain biker's most important piece of safety gear. To emphasize the importance of head protection, many bike shops are including helmets, helmet discounts, or other incentives with the purchase of a mountain bike. In any case, you should make sure a helmet is part of your overall bicycle budget. A ''brain bucket'' could save your life and should be considered a mandatory piece of equipment. It is among the best investments you can make to ensure a long and healthy life of mountain biking.

A helmet's main purpose is to reduce harmful effects of a blow to the head. Today's helmets are safe, sturdy, and lightweight, with most models weighing just 8 or 9 ounces (227 or 255 g). Expanded polystyrene (EPS) is the energy-absorbing material of which most helmets are made. A smaller number of helmets are made from expanded polypropylene. Helmets are covered with a thin plastic shell, hard plastic shell, or Lycra. Generally, the hard-shell models have been considered tougher and the foam models lighter. All good helmets will meet ANSI and SNELL safety standards. Modern helmets are often computer-designed to provide better fit and ventilation and reduced wind resistance.

Look for comfort, fit, light weight, ventilation, durability, and removable, adjustable padding. Quick release buckles are standard. Bright coloring will make you more visible to motorists (you can also pick up brightly colored and inexpensive helmet covers).

Helmet prices range from about $40 to $150, less for youngsters and more for top-rated competition models with features such as pump airflow fitting.

AT A GLANCE: HELMET SURFACES

	Advantages	*Disadvantages*	*Dollar range*
Hard plastic	Very durable Prevents penetration of sharp objects	Slightly heavier	$30-$60
Thin plastic	Attractive, durable, light, easy to clean	None	$40-$150
Lycra	Less expensive, can change cover	Harder to keep clean, can snag on limbs and branches	$30-$60

Helmets are available to fit every rider.

Wear your helmet and show your children, by example, the importance of head protection. Cyclists suffer far too many head injuries, and of those injuries 75 percent are in children younger than 15.

Even in this enlightened age, you may hear some cyclists suggest that helmets are hot, uncomfortable, and unnecessary. Don't believe it. You'll get used to your helmet quickly and it will be part of your everyday ride.

■ FIT YOUR HELMET PROPERLY

For proper safety, it is imperative that your helmet fit snugly. Follow these steps to make sure the fit of your helmet is correct.

1. Place the helmet on your head so that it rests low on the brow to protect your forehead.
2. Adjust the straps so they form a Y in front of and below the ear. The chin strap should fit well under the chin and against the neck to be as snug as possible. This will ensure that your helmet stays in place when you need it most.

3. With the helmet fastened, push the helmet backward and forward, side to side. If the skin on your brow moves with the helmet and if the helmet moves only slightly, the fit is good.

Eye Protection

Eye protection is often underrated in terms of safety. Serious eye injuries can occur to cyclists who do not use eye protection. One of the most serious is damage from the sun's ultraviolet rays. Most of today's modern cycling and skiing glasses offer 100 percent UV protection.

Another reason for wearing glasses is to protect your eyes from foreign objects such as rocks coming off your tires, insects, and branches of trees or bushes.

The best sunglasses are optically true. They should also be made of an unbreakable and scratch-resistant material. Glasses that resemble goggles afford the most wind and weather protection. These glasses help protect the eye from flying objects, no matter what the angle.

Skin Protection

Cyclists should be concerned about skin protection. A good sunblock with a sun protection factor (SPF) of 15 is advisable. The best sunblocks are water resistant. Put the sunblock on 15 to 20 minutes before going into the sun. If necessary, plan on more than one application if you will be out for more than an hour in sunny weather.

Also keep in mind that a good moisturizer for the skin is important both before and after rides. The sun and wind can have a definite aging effect which moisturizers can help alleviate.

Gloves

Cycling gloves are used for safety and comfort. A good cycling glove can help protect your hands from abrasions if you fall, and padded gloves will help absorb road shock. If your hands have a tendency to numb while riding (a common occurrence), you may want to look into gloves with a petroleum based, gel-like material to better absorb shock. Gloves will also help protect against blisters and calluses. Use fingerless models for most riding and full-finger gloves in cold weather.

Look for durable, machine-washable gloves with heavy-duty palms and reinforced thumb pads, in either leather or synthetics, with Velcro closures. Some gloves have a sewn-in terry cloth brow wipe, which is a very handy feature.

Apparel

Fashion is in, of course, and cycling clothing offers plenty of style. But while shopping, remember that cycle apparel is designed primarily for function. It pads you, protects you, and keeps you cool or warm, dry and comfortable, in sweltering or subfreezing conditions.

In cycling, the effects of changing temperatures can be dramatic. You may overheat on a long climb only to chill on a long, shaded descent. Sweat can turn to dampness, chill, and even hypothermia (a lowering of the body temperature). Rain and cold weather can put a damper on your riding if you're not properly attired. In winter, frostbite can affect the extremities. If you ride year-round, proper cycling apparel becomes a necessity.

As in other active outdoor endeavors, layering is the key to good cycling dress. A single summer layer is replaced by perhaps two layers during the changing seasons and three during the cold winter months.

DRESSING FOR SUCCESS

Bike Shorts and Tights

Bike shorts will probably become your first item of cycling apparel after a few hard days in the saddle. Tights serve the same purpose, but are used in colder temperatures to cover the entire leg. Both are usually made to fit the bent-leg cycling position. Look for comfort, durability, multipanel design, ample padding around the crotch, and heavy-duty stitching on either stretch Lycra (with leg gripper material to keep the short from riding up) or the baggy, mountain-bike-style short. Cycling shorts and tights have a longer rise than exercise garments for comfort and coverage in the cycling position. As an alternative, try padded cycling briefs (for men and women); then you can wear any shorts or pants and still enjoy a padded ride.

Shoes

Cycling shoes have a stiffer sole to put more power into your pedaling. Mountain bike shoes have a hiking-boot-style tread pattern for those times you must push or carry your bike. Many of the new cycling shoes for mountain biking and road biking are designed for use with either toe clip or step-in (clipless) pedals.

Jerseys and Jackets

Look for a garment that wicks moisture away from the skin (such as polypropylene, CoolMax, etc.). Modern materials allow cooling in hot weather yet preserve body heat in colder temperatures. Outside, you'll want rain and wind protection (Gore-Tex, Supplex, etc.). A long tail cut in back and longer sleeves provide body coverage in the bent-over riding position. Velcro closures, easy-to-reach pockets, venting, and bright colors are added features. Many cycling garments have sewn-in reflective materials to increase visibility.

All-Weather Suits

Look for Gore-Tex or a similar proven all-weather material. Multi-purpose suits should be fully ventilated with underarm zippers and back vents to control the amount of heat and vapor that will escape.

Look for long tails on the jacket, a high waist on the pants, leg zippers, and Velcro cuff closures.

A relatively mild day can bring a windchill factor of freezing if the wind is blowing briskly. Bundling up with heavy clothes is not the answer; your clothing can become wet or sweat-soaked. You can stay warm and dry by layering. It is important to have an undergarment that wicks moisture away from the skin. Your middle layer provides insulation, and your outer shell provides wind and rain protection. Materials such as Gore-Tex and Ultrex are breathable to wick away moisture yet provide excellent water repellency.

Remember, you can lose up to 40 percent of your body heat through your head. Headbands or ski hats can be worn under the helmet. A helmet cover can provide some protection. Use full-fingered, windproof, and waterproof cycling gloves. Too much glove padding (such as in ski gloves) can affect your ability to shift and brake. Use socks or neoprene covers (booties) over your cycling shoes. Stow away some polypropylene arm and leg warmers to pull on when the weather changes quickly.

Accessories

If your riding takes you more than walking distance from civilization, you should consider certain accessories for your mountain bike. In addition to basic items such as a water bottle, you may need a pump, patch kit, spare tire tube, and basic tools including Allen wrenches and a small crescent wrench. Remember, flat tires are by far the most common back-country breakdown mountain bikers face.

Water Bottles

A water bottle is the most common mountain bike accessory. In fact, many bikes come equipped with a water bottle cage attached to the frame. Many riders carry two bottles. Cages are made of various materials and new configurations are being introduced. Oversized cages will hold larger, 1.5-liter bottles for thirsty riders or long trips. Some riders use specially made belts or backpacks with a water bottle pocket; some have straws so you can sip and still keep both hands on your bars. Insulated under-seat packs are made to keep water bottles cold.

Pumps

Mountain bikers often prefer mini-pumps that can be attached to the down tube or top tube of the frame. One manufacturer has even designed a pump that is built into a sliding seat post. The larger, full-size pumps may pump more air per stroke but they are less handy. Hand-sized inflating devices that use replaceable CO_2 (carbon dioxide) cartridge refills can be used by the rider who wants to keep gear at a minimum. These can be carried in a pack or clipped to the frame. Good pumps are equipped for use with both Presta and Schrader valves. Look for durability, ease of use, and easy mounting.

Packs

Most popular is the seat pack which mounts under your saddle and is used for your tools, patch kit, and day-ride items. For the rider who wants to pack more or for the tourer, there are handlebar bags (some come with map mounts), panniers (paired for balanced load) for front and rear, and triangular frame bags that can carry small items and double as shoulder padding when you carry your bike. In all cycling packs, look for durable materials, balance, convenience, and easy access.

Luggage Racks

Without a rack, anything sizable is difficult to transport on a bicycle. It takes both hands and feet to ride safely. For trips to the post office or corner store, a rack is a nice addition. Look for strength, light weight, and the ability to carry a balanced load. Racks come in front and rear models. A rear rack should be used first; add a front rack for touring. Some newer racks come equipped with convenient built-in cargo straps, and some racks also offer mud protection.

Cycle Computers

Using a cycle computer adds a whole new dimension to your riding and training. You can time your rides and measure trip distance, total distance, current speed, and maximum speed. Better models also measure cadence and average speed (to let you know whether you're at your desired training level). Some also have altimeters that will show elevation changes on your ride. The latest, top-end models have built-in heart rate monitors.

Most models include clock, stopwatch, odometer, and speedometer (adjustable to miles or kilometers per hour) and automatic on/off. Cadence, altimeter, and heart rate functions are found in the pricier models.

Look for size of display, ease of use, watertightness, and light weight. Beware of wireless models; these may work well on road bikes but

Distribute your supplies evenly in panniers for comfortable touring.

sometimes don't stand up in rough off-road riding. In cycle computers, you can generally expect to get what you pay for. The expensive models work very well; the inexpensive models may be confusing to operate, inaccurate in measurement, and short-lived.

Mirrors

Safe riders are aware of their surroundings. Small mirrors that attach to the end of the handlebar and can be tucked away in tight riding conditions are among the best choices. Some riders prefer tiny models that attach to the helmet or eyeglasses.

Lights

With more night riding and mountain bike commuting, demand has increased for lights. Off-road lighting began with helmet lights similar to those used by coal miners, and they are still popular. Today's lighting choices are much wider and include battery-powered halogen headlamps and flashing or constant taillights. The lamps are clamped to the bike; the battery is either mounted to the frame or carried in a custom seat pack. Look for long-life rechargeability, weathertightness, and adjustability.

Mud Guards

If much of your riding is on muddy roads or trails, then, by all means, pick up some mud guards. They will prevent your legs, back, and usually your face from being splattered.

SAFETY TIP If you plan to ride in remote areas, you should be prepared to deal with any emergencies that may occur.

Compact first-aid kits can be purchased at cycling, sporting goods, auto parts, or camping and outdoor stores. They include basic materials to treat minor cuts and bruises and insect bites. Small kits will fit in a bag under your saddle.

3

MOUNTAIN BIKING CORRECTLY

The rewards of mountain biking are measured in many ways. One of the most satisfying is in adapting your riding style to the challenges that nature presents to you—in using the terrain for a graceful, flowing ride, no matter what the obstacles. This gives a sense of accomplishment and a oneness with your surroundings. Like the skier or sailor, the mountain biker picks a line and blends his or her movement to the challenge at hand.

Mountain biking is easy to learn; with practice, its techniques become instinctive. If you have ridden a bicycle, skillful mountain biking is mainly a matter of learning shifting, braking, and weight distribution techniques and, of course, developing a sufficient fitness level.

Like the powder skiers who carve graceful arcs in fresh snow, experienced mountain bikers embody grace and elegance as they put their unique touches on the landscape.

Meeting the challenges of nature.

Covering the terrain in good form.

Basic Braking, Shifting, and Body Position

On your first mountain bike ride, you will begin—as a matter of necessity—to develop the basic skills of braking and shifting. It's not hard to squeeze your brake levers or click your shifters, but it takes time and practice to learn the secrets of stopping powerfully and in balance on varied terrain or shifting fluidly at just the right time to carry the proper speed through a change in the trail.

Braking

The power of standard mountain bike cantilever brakes is limited mainly by how much energy it takes to use the brake lever. The cycling industry is developing many innovations in brakes. Self-energizing, hydraulic, and cam brake systems are being improved and may become more widely used in coming years. Much attention is being paid to advances such as these because more efficient braking will make off-road biking even more safe and enjoyable than it is today.

In braking, the general rule is to use the rear brake first. Too much pressure on the front brake could toss you onward without your bike. Also be aware of which hand controls which brake. Standard bikes are set up so the right hand controls the rear brake and the left hand controls the front brake. This works because the natural tendency for a right-handed person is to squeeze the rear brake first. Be sure to check any used bikes because some riders, mostly left-handers, do change the pattern because of personal preference. For simplicity's sake, southpaws can and should quickly get used to the standard brake setup.

Of course, using front and rear brakes together gives you the best stopping power. It must be emphasized, however, that too much front brake use can pitch you forward, so it is good to practice a slight rearward shift of the body as you increase pressure on the front brake. The rear brake is especially valuable in controlling speed at slower speeds, but above about 15 mph (24 kph), the rear brake may not stop you quickly enough on its own.

Practice brake use on a safe, level area to find the combination of stopping power that feels best for you. Make sure you can comfortably reach both brake levers and squeeze them effectively. Brake levers can be adjusted for reach so a person with a small hand can get a good grip, even on a large lever.

Practice routine stops and then work up to quicker stops. Avoid skidding except for an occasional test of your rear brake adjustment; your lever should be adjusted so you can lock and skid the rear wheel without the brake lever touching the handlebar.

Most brakes have barrel adjustments near the lever that can be easily used to set proper tension. You should also check to make sure your brake pads, front and rear, are hitting evenly on the rim and not rubbing on the tire. This can cause unnecessary tire damage.

Practice braking in all terrain and conditions. Remember that wet rims will inhibit stopping power by 10 to 30 percent so use extra caution in damp conditions. The idea is to be prepared to slow down or stop quickly in all conditions and in any emergency.

■ PRACTICE SAFE BRAKING

1. Find a safe, level area for braking practice. Start by practicing routine stops, then work up to quicker stops.
2. When you decide to stop, gently squeeze the rear brake first with your right hand.
3. Within a split second, gently squeeze the front brake lever with your left hand while shifting your weight slightly to the rear of the bike.
4. Remember that too much front brake might pitch you forward but that the back brake alone at speeds over 15 mph (24 kph) won't stop you quickly enough.

EARTH WATCH   The most serious environmental scars mountain bikers leave on trail systems occur when the rider skids his or her rear wheel in braking. Trail damage is also caused by riding during or right after a rain.

Good mountain bikers avoid causing erosion and unnecessary roughness on the trail. This is a growing concern among organized mountain bike groups, other trail users, and environmentalists.

Learn to brake and stop at a point just short of skidding. This is the most efficient way to apply the brakes, and it is much easier on nature.

Shifting

Shifting gears takes more practice than braking. Most mountain bikes have 15, 18, 21, or 24 speeds, so you will have plenty of choices. Your legs and gears together are like your car's transmission; they turn smoothly, at different cadences, depending on speed and terrain. Always keep pedaling as you shift gears. Smooth pedaling leads to smooth shifting.

Mountain bike gear-shifters are located so you can shift safely and easily without lifting your hands from the handlebar. There are different styles of shifters—including thumb-shift levers, push-button or rapid-fire shifters, and grip shifters in which the hand grip turns (like on a motorcycle throttle)—but all accomplish the same basic function: moving the chain from one chainring to another.

If you have thumb levers, think of shifting as clockwise and counterclockwise motions. To upshift you move your shifters clockwise, to downshift you move them counterclockwise (more on changing gears in a few paragraphs). This goes for either hand; think of your handlebar as the face of a clock, or a steering wheel.

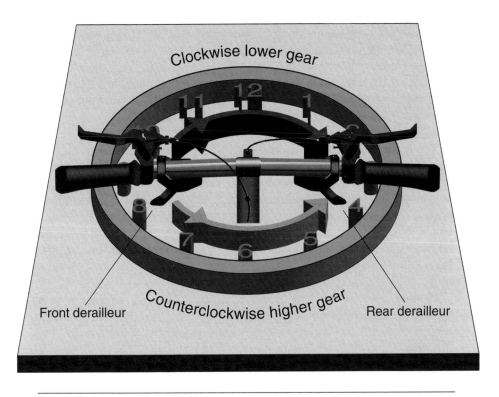

Thumb levers.

■ LEARN TO SHIFT EFFICIENTLY

With practice, you'll soon learn how to find the gear that works best for the terrain you're riding. While you're learning, remember these tips.

1. Shift one gear at a time, shifting the front first, then rear.
2. As you approach an ascent, you should move from the larger chainring to the smaller. Upshift as you approach a descent.
3. Maintain a consistent pedal cadence as you shift gears.

Body Position

Frame size, seat height, and reach each have an effect on basic body position and comfort on the mountain bike. Your bike should not be too big. Be sure you can straddle the bike's top tube with comfortable clearance; experts often will recommend 2 inches (5 cm) of clearance if you plan on-road riding and up to 4 inches (10 cm) for off-road riding. A more general rule of thumb is 2 inches (5 cm) of clearance for a recreational rider and 4 inches (10 cm) for a more aggressive or competitive rider.

■ ADJUST YOUR SADDLE HEIGHT

The optimal saddle height depends on whether you are pedaling normally or descending a steep hill. Some riders lower their seat a few inches on tough descents for safety and stability. Because most mountain bikes are equipped with quick-release seat posts, you can quickly slide your saddle up or down as the terrain dictates. To adjust your saddle height to the optimal position for pedaling normally, use this process:

1. Sit on the seat.
2. Loosen the seat post and slide it up until your leg is outstretched with your heel on the pedal.
3. Make sure that your leg is slightly bent when the ball of your foot is centered on the pedal.

Proper reach will put you in a comfortable, powerful position, neither too outstretched nor too upright, with arms slightly bent, not locked. In the riding position, your back should be at about a 45-degree angle. To accomplish this position, your handlebar will be slightly lower than your

The handlebars should be slightly lower than the seat; this should put your back at a 45-degree angle.

saddle. As you bend over into a more aggressive position, you have more leverage and balance. If you sit too straight, you may sacrifice power.

Depending on how aggressively you ride, you may want to experiment with the height and length of your handlebar stem. Raising the stem will put you in a more upright position, which is usually more comfortable but less powerful. Lowering the stem will lower your upper body and probably reduce your comfort but give you more leverage and power. Lower-priced bikes will usually have higher stems and more upright riding positions. More expensive bikes, especially competition models, will have lower stems to distribute the rider's weight forward for leverage, power, and control.

Riding Uphill

Uphill riding skills involve shifting, weight distribution, balance, and momentum. You must be able to judge degrees of steepness, surface conditions, and obstacle clearance.

■ HANDLE CLIMBS EFFECTIVELY

The first thing to remember as you approach a hill is to shift down into a smaller gear well ahead of time, before you roll to a stop. It's not necessary to shift all the way down, but knowing you can get down into the right gear is important. Plan ahead and you won't lose momentum when you really need it. Here's how to approach a hill with confidence:

1. When you're almost to the hill, first shift off of your big chainring in front to the middle chainring with your left hand.
2. Glance down between your feet to check which ring your chain is on, then quickly look back to the trail.
3. If things look steep, shift again, this time from the middle to the small chainring.
4. If pedal speed is dropping, shift your rear derailleur into one of the middle cogs with your right hand. Keep shifting down until you find the right gear for you.
5. Don't wait too long to change gears. Shifting becomes more difficult as pedal speed drops.
6. Keep your weight balanced by bending at the waist and elbows to shift some of your weight over the front wheel while you're seated.
7. Watch for rocks, ruts, or other obstacles so you can plan ahead for proper pedal clearance.

Your effort should be based on how long the hill appears to be. When climbing, it is wiser to choose too small a gear than too large. In a low gear, your feet will spin rapidly, but this uses less energy than pushing harder in a higher gear.

In the proper gear, you can prepare for the tough part of the climb. Concentration is important in two ways. You must believe you are going to stay on your bike to the top of the hill and, depending on the terrain, you must look ahead for the proper line. This simply means that if there are rocks, ruts, curbs, or a combination of these, you must choose the easiest and most ridable line. Concentrate on what is directly ahead of you, yet glance beyond as well. Plan ahead and you will avoid coming to a sudden stop.

Weight Distribution

When climbing a steep hill, you must balance your weight properly. Normally, you will be seated as you climb. This means your weight will

Sports File/Tim Hancock

Bend your arms and press some weight forward to prevent tipping over backward when going uphill.

be over the rear wheel to maintain good traction. At the same time, you must keep the front of the bike weighted. This is done partly by flattening your back and bending your elbows to press weight forward. Being too far back could cause the front wheel to rise and even cause you to tip over backward.

If you find it necessary to stand up for more power as you climb a hill, you may have to shift your weight back some to maintain traction. By slightly shifting your weight up and back you will find the position that will allow you to stand and pedal without breaking traction.

It is always a challenge to see whether you can stay on the bike as you go up a very steep trail, but remember, those slow-motion falls can really hurt! If it looks too steep, plan ahead and get off and walk. Many riders have fallen hard because they were stubborn and waited too long to dismount.

The idea is to have fun and enjoy yourself, not to accidentally roll off a steep embankment. Keep this in mind and know your limitations.

Pedal Clearance

It's important to know your pedal clearance. When your pedal is down you have very limited ground clearance. If you are riding over a rock, rut, or other obstacle be careful not to bury your pedal. This can lead to another slow motion fall and damage to you, your bike, or both.

Some hills require a short burst of pedal speed so that you will be able to put your pedal in the proper horizontal position to make it over a tricky obstacle. Also, because most hills have one or several steep pitches, you may need to pedal quickly to negotiate the steep parts, then rest on the flatter sections.

Thoughts on Climbing

Make sure you are completely in gear before you put maximum load on the pedals. Try to remain seated when climbing steep, loose sections. Standing up in loose areas is a sure way to lose traction and come to an unnecessary stop.

Keep in mind that wet tires, rocks, and wood are very slippery. Having a little less air pressure in your tires will give better traction. Keeping your toe clip straps a little loose or the tension light on clipless pedals when climbing hills will help you dismount quickly and smoothly.

It helps to take a hill little by little. That is, don't come to the base of a climb and look way up to the top and say, "I know I can't make this hill." Surprise yourself by taking it one short section at a time. Before you know it, you'll be at the top. But always remember, hills will get your heart pumping in a hurry. Pay attention to your body. If your heart is pounding in your ears, it's probably time to get off and walk or rest.

The main points to remember in climbing: Shift early so you will be in a low gear as you ride to the first steep pitch; keep your weight evenly distributed and stay seated on the really steep sections for better traction; slide back in the saddle for better leverage and traction; pick the proper line; watch your pedal clearance; anticipate when it is too steep and time to walk so you can dismount easily and avoid a nasty tumble.

See you at the top!

Riding Downhill

One of mountain biking's greatest thrills is the descent. Like the skier, the accomplished mountain bike rider blends her or his technique with the terrain, making each hill a new challenge, dancing with nature. Many basic riding skills come into play as you roll down a winding dirt road or steep trail.

SAFETY TIP   As we consider the elements involved in a descent, the most important factor, as in all riding, is safety. Never attempt a radical maneuver without practice at the most basic level and never let your riding companions persuade you to ride faster than your own judgment and abilities allow.

Downhill skills mainly involve braking and weight distribution. You must be able to judge steepness, surface conditions, and proper clearance of obstacles.

Easy Brake Test

First, test your brakes on easy downhill terrain. This will familiarize you with your estimated stopping distance. Remember, the front brake is your most powerful; used improperly, it could launch you through the air! The best stop is through combined use of the front and rear brakes. On a descent, the rear brake is often used to control speed.

After you have developed a feeling for brake use and stopping power, you are ready to test yourself on a descent. Find an easy hill and ride it a few times, practicing your braking and weight distribution.

Braking efficiency and weight distribution are related; if your weight is back as you go down a hill, you will have more weight on both wheels and therefore more stopping power when you apply the brakes of both wheels.

Try this test at a slow speed and then faster after you gain confidence. While riding slowly down a hill, squeeze the front brake twice as hard as you squeeze the rear brake. Your body weight will immediately shift forward, possibly unweighting the rear wheel. This can cause a loss of control. When your rear wheel starts to jump or skid, let up on the front brake. Force your weight back by shifting your rear end over or behind the seat while standing on the pedals with your cranks in a horizontal position. This technique will help you slow down and greatly shorten your stopping distance. Practice this weight shift until you always feel in control.

David Epperson

Standing on the pedals and shifting your rear end over the seat will help you maintain control during descents.

Keep in mind that as you apply either brake the effect is to transfer your weight forward. Move your body weight back, sometimes even behind the seat. This will stop you faster and might save you from a spill.

Visualize yourself during this braking exercise. Your cranks are horizontal, your weight is evenly distributed, knees and elbows are bent to absorb any bumps, your head is up, eyes are looking ahead, and you are poised to steer in either direction and react quickly to any change in the terrain. An added advantage is that in this position your horizontal cranks have the greatest ground clearance over obstacles.

More Advanced Braking

After practicing basic braking on smooth, wide descents, you can test your skills on a tougher hill. For steep descents on either roads or single-track trails, more advanced techniques are needed.

On the steeps, the front brake is used with extreme care. Some good riders use it very little. You should learn to modulate your front brake, using it in conjunction with your rear brake and applying it for only a split second at a time to help control speed. Remember, your front wheel needs to keep rolling and steering, no matter how slowly, or you will definitely be on your way to a face-plant.

For really hairy descents, many advanced riders lower their seat height to allow them to get way back—with their stomachs near or actually on the saddle—to increase braking power.

On steep descents, keep your weight over the rear wheel and use the front brake sparingly.

■ MASTER DESCENTS

The new rider must always know how efficiently he or she can stop before attempting any descent. While your stopping power is controlled mainly by squeezing the brake levers for your front and rear brakes, body positioning is also important.

1. Prepare to descend by shifting up until you can maintain control of the pedals. If the descent is steep, lower your seat so you can shift your weight to the rear.
2. Squeeze the front and rear brakes. When your rear wheel starts to jump or skid, let up on the front brake. If the descent is very steep and fast, use the front brake only a split second at a time.
3. Force your weight back by shifting your rear end over or behind the seat when standing on the pedals with the cranks in a horizontal position.

Cornering

Cornering, especially at speed or on steeper downhills, often requires that you keep your outside pedal down. This is important for two reasons. It gives you the best pedal clearance on the inside of the turn and it counterbalances your bike and body. In some instances you will put some additional weight on the outside pedal as you enter the turn.

There are different ways to steer your bike through corners. You should attempt to lean the bike and your body by turning your hips into the corner; this is especially important for beginners who will quickly find this to be smoother and safer than turning the handlebars and risking a sudden spill. First lean the bike into the turn and then fine-tune the turn with body lean. If you lean your body too much in the early stages of a turn, the front wheel can wash out, and it will be difficult to tighten up a corner. It is easier to avoid a fall by not overcommitting the lean angle of your bike. Remember, if you enter a corner faster than you want and don't think you can make the turn, lean more. If the bike washes out, at

Always have your inside foot ready on the turn.

least you don't ride off an embankment or into the trees. Practice steering from the hips and leaning the bike more than your body.

You should always have your inside foot ready to catch yourself in case you lean too much on a turn. If you use toe clips, you might kick out or loosen them for a tough turn or descent. Always remember to let your bike roll through the apex of the turn—the tightest part, where you're leaning the most. It's easy to break loose if you brake in the turn. Reduce your chance of falling by braking hard before the turn, slowing to a comfortable speed, and then riding through the turn. If you don't let go of the brakes a little, you can't turn because there will likely be too much weight on the front wheel.

If the trail or road is either very loose or wet, be extra cautious with your front brake. This caution is needed because in loose dirt or gravel your rear wheel is likely to slide away from you. If it's wet, your brakes are more likely to grab.

■ LEARN TO TURN CORNERS SAFELY

Good preparation is the key to cornering.

1. Keep your outside pedal in a down position.
2. Shift your hips and lean your bike into the turn. Body lean can be used to fine-tune your turning.
3. Slow down early so your bike can roll through the apex of the turn.
4. If you use toe clips, kick out or loosen them when conditions are very difficult.

Handling Terrain Changes

Whenever you're riding off-road, you must be prepared to recognize and negotiate obstacles. These challenges may include ruts, logs, rocks, streams, curbs, or culverts.

Clearances are of most importance to the fast or downhill rider. You have to know what size obstacle can be crossed before your pedals or chainrings will hit. You can come to a very costly and abrupt stop if you misjudge. If you are unsure in approaching an obstacle, it is best to stop and check it out. Dismounting and rolling your bike over the object will help you determine clearance. Then, you can always go back and ride over it.

When crossing large ruts or culverts, never hit your front brake when dropping in. This can stop your front wheel and send you onward without

Riding the ruts in Durango, Colorado.

your bike. Besides the accident, major damage to your frame, fork, or wheel is a possibility. If you're not sure, again, walk it through the first time. Soon you will come to obstacles that appear impossible, but you will discover that you can ride them. But take your time.

When riding a particularly rutted road or trail, keep your vision focused well ahead of you. Ruts can be very tricky; you may need to roll in or out at an opportune time to avoid major drop-offs or unpassable sections. Sometimes it's best to ride in the ruts; sometimes it's better to skirt the ruts. Sometimes you get in a rut and can't get out.

Avoid rocks when possible. In rough, rocky sections, ride with weight evenly distributed. Look for the least rock-strewn line. Sharp rocks cause more flat tires on mountain bikes than perhaps any other obstacle.

Watch for deep sand. It can stop you dead in your tracks. Stay seated and let the bike roll through a sandy section. Try to ride the more packed section or skirt the sandy area altogether for better traction. (Hint: Riding in sandy, saltwater areas can cause corrosion to your equipment, so wash your bike afterward.)

In summary, let safety be your guide as you roll down hills and through the many challenges in terrain. The more you ride, the more confidence you will gain. While descending, shift up in anticipation of the hill ahead, use your brakes in combination, and keep your body weight back. Always be aware of possible oncoming traffic. Never ride faster than you feel is safe, and never let your friends dictate the pace.

See you at the bottom!

David Epperson

Riding on packed sand makes for easier pedaling.

Crossing Water

Water crossings can be an exciting test of skill, determination, and judgment, plus they can be very refreshing during a hot ride. But always use caution. As you approach a creek bed, look for the shallowest area. To keep your feet dry, keep your cranks horizontal. This, of course, is not always possible—sometimes you'll have to pedal through the crossing and it may be deeper than pedal level.

Carry good momentum into the stream but always be on the lookout for large rocks or other submerged obstacles that could impede your progress. If you need to pedal, stay seated for better traction and stability.

On your stream approach, be sure to shift to a smaller gear—if you can't coast through, at least you'll be in a lower gear and ready to pedal so you won't bog down in midstream. If you cannot see the bottom because of muddy water, take extra care or avoid entirely if possible.

Did you make it across? Good job. Now you can watch your friends to see whether they pedal or paddle.

David Epperson

Getting across water is a fun challenge.

■ CROSS WATER SKILLFULLY

1. Look for the shallowest area of water.
2. Keep your cranks horizontal if you can coast through the water.
3. Shift to a lower gear if you can't coast through the water.
4. Stay seated for good traction and stability.

Carrying Your Bike

When it is time to dismount and carry your bike, try this safe and easy carrying technique. Standing on the left of your bike (you don't want to get greasy from your chain or chainrings), put your right arm through the frame, reach around, grab the handlebar and pull it toward you.

The bike will rest on your right shoulder where the top tube and the seat tube meet. Or you can simply hoist your bike onto your right shoulder balancing it with your right hand under the top tube.

When it's impossible to keep riding, the shoulder carry is an effective way to get your bike over obstacles.

The shoulder carry is a relatively comfortable carrying method for people of all shapes and sizes. It is more difficult to carry a traditional women's-style bike; this is one reason why many women ride men's models.

Always keep your left hand free for balance. If you carry your bike a great deal, get a portage strap or add padding so your load will be more comfortable on your shoulder.

Outdoor Awareness and Trail Etiquette

The mountain bike allows more people than ever before to enjoy scenic outdoor and wilderness areas. Ridden carefully, a mountain bike will leave few imprints on pristine wilderness areas. Like the backpacker who leaves only footprints, the aware mountain bike rider leaves nothing more than a tire track.

Outdoor awareness, courtesy, and safe riding practices are essential if mountain bike riders hope to continue to share trails with other outdoor enthusiasts. Mountain biking's continued growth and reputation will be determined in large part by the image projected by today's riders. Unsafe, selfish use of trails, more than anything else, will spoil public land use and limit access for future generations of mountain bike riders.

Already, trails in some heavily used areas have been closed to mountain bike riders. Some of the closures are due to rude behavior and lack of respect on the part of unthinking riders. On the positive side, mountain bike groups have opened trails after demonstrating commitment to trail sharing and environmental awareness. Many mountain bike clubs are building and maintaining trails as community service projects.

Although mountain bikes are quiet, low-impact vehicles, they can be used in a manner threatening to other trail users. We must respect the

Respectfully yielding the right of way to other trail users in the San Juan Mountains of Colorado.

rights of hikers, horseback riders, and nature lovers. Each type of use has its place. If you're riding through a scenic mountain area frequented by bird-watchers or other wildlife observers, it is obviously best to ride slowly and quietly. A friendly, low-volume bell on your handlebar can be used to signal your approach in a quiet manner. Save your fast action for a place where others won't be bothered. We must be careful not to disturb wildlife in our riding areas. Since mountain bikers are among the newest additions to the list of wilderness users, we must be careful to show that we are good neighbors, that we are safe and responsible riders.

Many of us think that mountain bikes can be less damaging to the environment than horses. They can bring wilderness enjoyment to more people and, as a result, help build more support for resource conservation efforts. Although there have been a few complaints about mountain bike damage to trail systems, there is no scientific proof that mountain bikers cause any more environmental damage than other trail users.

When it comes to outdoor awareness, the message should be clear to all mountain bikers: Ride safely, courteously, and responsibly. Otherwise, all mountain bikers may pay the price of an irresponsible few.

EARTH WATCH   Responsible mountain bikers . . .

. . . don't trespass.

. . . don't litter.

. . . don't ride through wet meadows.

. . . ride at safe speeds.

. . . respect private property.

IMBA RULES OF THE TRAIL

1. Ride on open trails only. Respect trail and road closures (ask if you're not sure), avoid possible trespass on private land, obtain permits and authorization as may be required. Federal and state wilderness areas are closed to cycling.
2. Leave no trace. Be sensitive to the dirt beneath you. Even on open trails, you should not ride under conditions where you will leave evidence of your passing, such as on certain soils shortly after a rain. Observe the different types of soils and trail construction; practice low-impact cycling. This also means staying on the trail and not creating any new ones. Be sure to pack out at least as much as you pack in.
3. Control your bicycle. Inattention for even a second can cause problems. Obey all speed laws.
4. Always yield the trail. Make known your approach well in advance. A friendly greeting (or a bell) is considerate and works well; don't startle others. Show your respect when passing others by slowing to a walk or even stopping. Anticipate that other trail users may be around corners or in blind spots.
5. Never spook animals. All animals are startled by an unannounced approach, a sudden movement, or a loud noise. This can be dangerous for you, for others, and for the animals. Give animals

extra room and time to adjust to you. When passing horses, use special care and follow the rider's directions (as if you're uncertain). Running cattle and disturbing wild animals is a serious offense. Leave gates as you found them, or as marked.

6. Plan ahead. Know your equipment, your ability, and the area in which you are riding—and prepare accordingly. Be self-sufficient at all times. Wear a helmet, keep your machine in good condition, and carry necessary supplies for changes in weather or other conditions. A well-executed trip is a satisfaction to you and not a burden or offense to others.

4

HEALTHY AND SAFE MOUNTAIN BIKING

Few outdoor pursuits compare with mountain biking to combine adventure, fun, and fitness. No matter where you live or how you ride, you can increase your fitness level, feel better about yourself, and add new vigor to your life.

Each time you hop on your bike, you will be able to seek out new challenges to your riding abilities and at the same time improve your strength, flexibility, and cardiorespiratory system.

Mountain biking is the sport for many of us who want to improve our physical condition but find repetitive indoor exercises to be tedious. Pumping iron or pedaling a stationary bicycle might make us stronger, but sweating in a gym can't match the excitement of blue sky, fresh air, and the great outdoors.

As we ride mountain bikes, we are able to let the adventuresome spirit inside of us escape and come out to play. At the same time we can develop a youthful vitality, possibly adding years to our lives through increased strength, endurance, and cardiorespiratory fitness.

And because we are able to explore some very beautiful places, mountain biking also allows peace of mind and mental relaxation—stress reduction, if you prefer. During your rides you may work out personal and family issues and develop creative new solutions to business or career challenges you have been thinking about.

Contemplating new horizons—one of the rewards of mountain biking.

How Ready Is Your Body?

You don't need to be in top physical shape to take up mountain biking. Cycling is an activity that nearly everyone can pursue, regardless of age. If you enjoy a brisk walk, you will enjoy a brisk ride. Certainly if you do ride your mountain bike regularly, you will improve your physical condition, especially your heart and lung capacity.

One of the most appealing aspects of cycling is that it's gentle on the body—a nonimpact form of exercise. It is perhaps one of the most exciting activities that does not put heavy impacts on the athlete's knees, ankles, or back. Of course, cycling can be extremely demanding, depending on conditions and terrain. But in cycling you are much less likely than in other activities to be sore or unable to exercise for days afterward because of aching muscles or joints. This is an important attraction for many people who must limit jarring exercise because of age or injury.

Another attraction of cycling is that each rider may choose his or her own level of participation and energy output. This is one of the reasons cycling, particularly mountain biking, is gaining converts from other activities such as running, tennis, and skiing. The low risk of injury and high fitness benefit are tough to match.

Mountain biking provides a good workout, and each rider can set her own pace.

Before taking up mountain biking, or any other active pursuit, you should get approval from your personal physician. This is most important for middle-aged and older people who want to adopt a more active lifestyle. If you want to enjoy the activity as well as receive its health benefits, it's always wise to know your starting point.

If you've ever ridden a bike, you can ride a mountain bike. If you have doubts about your physical condition or endurance level, cycling is good because you can take it easy the first time out and then increase time and distance at your own pace.

Find an initial off-road adventure that is not too hilly or tough to ride. The terrain you choose will definitely determine your enjoyment level. First-timers should seek out graded or groomed trails or dirt roads. If the route can be traveled by a motor vehicle, it is probably not overly steep. The next step up would typically be a fire road or double-track trail. Survey the horizon, estimate elevations, and decide whether you're ready for something steeper. The most difficult and technically demanding riding will be found on single-track trails and in the more mountainous areas. Use extreme caution when entering expert terrain for the first time. Advanced riding skills, balance, and top physical conditioning are recommended.

Your community bike shop can direct you to the nearby trails best suited to your physical condition and riding ability.

Improving Your Mountain Biking Fitness

Although you can enjoy a first moderate outing without a high level of physical fitness, the fitter you are, the more you'll be able to enjoy mountain biking. As your flexibility, strength, and cardiorespiratory fitness increase, you'll be able to ride longer, ride farther, and handle tougher terrains.

Basic Stretching Guidelines and Exercises for Cyclists

It is always a good idea to stretch your muscles before and after riding. Bob and Jean Anderson, authors of *Stretching* recommend these guidelines and stretches for bikers.[1]

> Stretching should be done slowly without bouncing. Stretch to where you feel a slight, easy stretch. Hold this feeling for 5 to 30 seconds. Hold only stretch tensions that feel good to you. The key to stretching is to be relaxed while you concentrate on the area being stretched. Your breathing should be slow, deep, and rhythmical. Don't worry about how far you can stretch. Stretch relaxed, and limberness will become just one of the many by-products of regular stretching.

----

[1]*Note.* Text excerpted from *Cycling Stretches*, © 1992 (22-1/2'' × 34'' poster) by Bob and Jean Anderson. Reprinted by permission. For a free catalog, write to Stretching, Inc., P.O. Box 767, Palmer Lake, CO 80133, or call 1-800-333-1307.

CALF STRETCH   Stand a little way from a solid support and lean on it with your forearms, your head resting on your hands. Bend one leg and place your foot on the ground in front of you leaving the other leg straight behind you. Slowly move your hips forward until you feel a stretch in the calf of your straight leg. Be sure to keep the heel of the foot of the straight leg on the ground and your toes pointed straight ahead. Hold an easy stretch for 30 seconds. Do not bounce. Stretch both legs.

CALF STRETCH

HAMSTRING AND LOWER BACK STRETCH   Sit on the floor and straighten your right leg. Put the sole of your left foot next to the inside of your straightened leg. Lean slightly forward from the hips and stretch the hamstrings of your right leg. Find an easy stretch and relax. If you can't touch your toes comfortably, hook a towel around your foot to help you stretch. Hold for 30 seconds. Do not lock your knee. Your right quadriceps should be soft and relaxed during the stretch. Keep your right foot upright with the ankle and toes relaxed. Repeat the stretch with your left leg.

HAMSTRING AND LOWER BACK STRETCH

ARMS, SHOULDERS, AND UPPER BACK STRETCH   Hold on to your bike. With your hands shoulder-width apart on this support, relax, keeping your arms straight and your chest moving downward and your feet remaining directly under your hips. Keep your knees slightly bent. Hold this stretch 30 seconds. Remember to always bend your knees when coming out of this stretch.

ARMS, SHOULDERS, AND UPPER BACK STRETCH

QUADRICEPS AND KNEE STRETCH While standing, grab the top of your right foot (from inside of foot) with your left hand and gently pull, moving your heel toward your buttocks. The knee bends at a natural angle in this position and creates a good stretch in the knee and quads. Hold for 30 seconds. Do both legs.

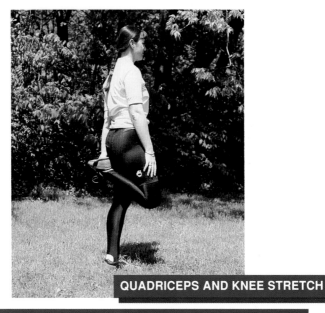

QUADRICEPS AND KNEE STRETCH

ACHILLES TENDONS, GROIN, LOWER BACK, AND HIPS STRETCH

With your feet shoulder-width apart and pointed out to about a 15-degree angle, heels on the ground, bend your knees and squat. If you have trouble staying in this position, hold on to something for support. Hold the stretch for 30 seconds. Be careful if you have had any knee problems. If pain is present, discontinue this stretch.

ACHILLES TENDONS, GROIN, LOWER BACK, AND HIPS STRETCH

Warming Up and Cooling Down

The first 10 to 20 minutes of riding is the warm-up phase. The warm-up should be a prelude to every ride. Pace yourself and take some time reaching your fastest pace.

At the end of each ride comes the cool-down—10 to 15 minutes of reduced energy output. The warm-up will help prevent injuries and the cool-down will help speed your recovery time from the ride. The warm-up and cool-down should be a regular beginning and end to your rides.

Cardiorespiratory Fitness

Cardiorespiratory fitness is the most important physical benefit you can achieve from mountain biking. The higher your cardiorespiratory fitness, the more you will be able to enjoy your mountain bike.

One way to get an idea of your level of cardiorespiratory fitness is to listen to your body as you ride. If you become winded or can't carry on a conversation with your fellow riders, you're probably riding too hard. Slow down and look for a comfortable rhythm.

Another way to check your cardiorespiratory fitness is to monitor your heart rate. And checking your pulse before, during, and after your rides will allow you to chart progress. After a few weeks or months of riding you will find marked improvement, especially in your heart recovery rate after a spurt of effort.

You can use the gears on your mountain bike as a factor in determining how much energy you expend during a ride. Depending on the surface you're riding on, you might try a pedal cadence in the range of 75 revolutions per minute. This rate is generally effective for improving cardiorespiratory fitness. Always try to turn the pedals with a fluid motion and to develop a feeling for applying pressure throughout the pedal stroke.

Getting Your Muscles Ready for Riding

Regular riding will allow you to gradually improve your muscular strength, and as your strength increases you'll be able to ride farther, higher, and longer. Take it easy at first. Don't try to ride 10 miles (16 km) of tough trails your first time out. Let your body be your guide to how hard you push yourself. If you want some added help in improving your muscular strength so you can enjoy those steeper hills and rougher trails, try some resistance training. We explain a few exercises, which use only your body weight to provide the resistance, that will strengthen your whole body. Perhaps surprisingly, your upper body strength has a big effect on your hill-climbing ability.

USE HEART RATE TO GAUGE
CARDIORESPIRATORY FITNESS

Specialists in sports medicine generally agree that to receive benefits from aerobic exercise such as cycling, you must work hard enough to get your heart pumping at 60 percent to 85 percent of your maximum heart rate and maintain this pace for 20 minutes to 30 minutes per workout. Here's how to determine your target heart rate range and how to check your pulse:

Finding Your Target Heart Rate Range

1. Subtract your age from 220 to calculate your approximate maximum heart rate.
2. Multiply your approximate maximum heart rate by 0.6 to find your lower heart rate target.
3. Multiply your approximate maximum heart rate by 0.85 to find your upper heart rate target.*

To get health benefits, your heart rate during aerobic exercise should fall between the upper and lower limits you just calculated.

Determining Your Heart Rate

1. Locate your pulse by pressing gently with your index and middle fingers at the base of your wrist or at the side of your neck near the Adam's apple.
2. Count the number of beats you feel in 15 seconds.
3. Multiply your 15-second count by 4 to determine your heart rate in beats per minute.

*You should talk with your doctor about this range if you take heart or blood pressure medicine. The medication may dictate that you use a lower heart rate range.

Start out trying to do 3 sets of 10 repetitions of each exercise. If you can't do that many, do what you can and increase the number of reps or sets as you feel you're ready.

DIPS You'll need two sturdy chairs with seats the same height for this exercise. Place them, seats facing each other, about 4 or 5 feet (1.2-1.5 m) apart (you may need to adjust this distance depending on your height). Place your hands on the edge of one chair seat, and your feet on the seat of the second chair. Lower yourself slowly, then straighten your elbows completely to lift yourself.

DIPS

PARTIAL SIT-UP Lie on your back on the floor with your knees bent, feet flat on the floor, and arms crossed over your chest. Press your lower back against the floor. Raise your shoulder blades off the floor by curling your head and shoulders up and forward until you can touch your knees with your hands. Hold this position for 2 or 3 seconds, then return your shoulders and head to the floor.

PARTIAL SIT-UP

PUSH-UPS Lie on your stomach with your palms flat on the floor about shoulder-width apart and your toes pointing down. Straighten your arms to lift your body, being sure to keep your back straight. You should be looking at the floor slightly in front of your hands. Keep your back straight, and lower your body by bending at the elbows until your chest touches the floor.

You can make this exercise easier by placing your knees on the floor instead of your toes. You can make the exercise harder by moving your hands wider apart.

PUSH-UPS

SQUAT   Stand with your feet flat on the floor about shoulder-width apart and your toes pointing straight forward. Bend at the knees and hips until your thighs are parallel to the floor, making sure your feet stay flat and your head stays upright. Putting your arms straight out in front of you as you bend may make balancing easier. Straighten your knees and hips to return to the starting position.

SQUAT

CALF RAISES Stand up straight with your feet on the floor and your arms at your sides. Rise onto your toes as far as you can, then slowly lower yourself.

To make this exercise harder, you can stand on the edge of a step (only your toes are on the step). Be sure to hold on to the handrail if you do this. You can also do this exercise on a step using only one leg at a time.

CALF RAISES

Energy Tips

You'll ride better and stronger if your body is properly fueled for the outing. This goes for both solid and liquid fuel.

Learn to recognize the benefits of simple and complex carbohydrates, the best source of energy for mountain biking or any other prolonged physical exercise. Look for fiber, grains, and vegetables when fueling up. Avoid large quantities of fats and proteins before a ride; they will serve only to slow you down in digestion time and energy output.

It's important to keep well hydrated when riding. Many riders will use 12 to 16 ounces (.35 to .47 liters) of water per hour, even in cooler conditions. It's a good idea to carry two water bottles on longer rides—with water in one and a premixed energy drink in the other. This combination will help keep you from dehydrating and losing energy. Find a carbo drink that pleases your taste buds and be sure to mix it properly. Too concentrated a mixture is hard to digest and may cause higher blood sugar and stomach upset.

Always bring along something solid to munch if you're planning to ride for more than an hour.

Always carry plenty of liquids with you on your rides.

Maintaining Your Bike for Safe Riding

A well-maintained mountain bike is essential to safe and worry-free riding. A poorly adjusted brake, loose connection, or other equipment failure can cause accident or injury.

You do not have to be mechanically inclined; mountain bikes are easy to understand and low in maintenance. You should learn the basics of cable adjustments and be prepared to repair a flat tire in off-road situations.

Barrel Cable Adjustments

It is not uncommon for new brake and shifter cables to stretch and need adjustment after a few weeks or months of riding. If you are on the trail and your brake levers suddenly squeeze all the way to your handlebar, you will definitely want to know how to adjust them.

Take a moment to inspect the barrel cable adjustments on your hand brake levers and shifters and ask for an adjustment demonstration at your

On-the-trail maintenance.

bike shop. Cables are easily adjusted on most newer bikes; many can be adjusted as you ride, without even stopping.

Lubrication

Lubrication should be applied lightly and at regular intervals to the chain and all pivot points on the derailleurs and shifting levers. Try to use a lube designed for mountain bikes. These lubes are designed to work better in the wetter and dirtier conditions found in off-road riding. If you ride in moderately wet conditions, you should have a shop repack your hubs, bottom bracket, and headset every year or two, unless you own a bike with sealed bearings that can't be serviced. This will increase the life of your bike dramatically. Have your bike shop advise you on what service is needed for sealed bearings.

Tools You May Need

A compact set of Allen wrenches and a small crescent wrench will allow you to work with just about every fitting on your bike.

Carrying a chain tool with extra chain pins will allow you to make on-trail chain repairs. A spoke wrench may be needed on rare occasions to tighten or loosen wheel spokes.

Carry a few zip ties. They can be used like baling wire for emergency repairs.

■ FIX A FLAT TIRE

Your saddle pack repair kit should include a spare inner tube, a patch kit, duct tape, and tire levers. You should also carry a pump.

If you have a flat tire, pull over and be sure you are out of the way of other cyclists or vehicles before starting the repairs.

1. Undo the yoke to the brake, undo the wheel's quick release, and remove the wheel. If it is a rear tire, shift to the smallest cog first so the wheel will slide out easier.
2. Visually inspect the tire for the cause of the flat. If the tire is severely damaged, it may not be fixable.
3. To repair, brace the wheel between your legs, with the valve at the bottom. At the top, insert the tire levers under the tire bead, about 6 inches (15 cm) apart. Use the levers individually to pry a 6-inch (15-cm) section of tire off the rim. Now remove the tire from one side of the rim and remove the tube.
4. Run your finger carefully around the inside of the tire to check for a protruding object. Watch for sharp objects such as thorns, nails, or glass. Remove the object. If your tread or sidewall is cut or gashed, repair from the inside using duct tape.
5. If you're patching a tube, find the hole, buff around the hole with your kit's sandpaper, partially inflate, add glue, let dry for a few minutes, then press on the patch.
6. Partially inflate your spare or repaired tube to give it shape. Insert the valve in the rim and fit the tube into the tire. Then starting at the valve, work the bead back on the rim. Thumb pressure usually works. You may have to use tire levers for the last 6 to 8 inches (15 to 20 cm). Be careful that you don't puncture the tube.
7. Fully inflate the tire with your pump, checking to see that the tire is seated evenly. Put the wheel back on, fasten the quick release, and reattach the brake yoke piece.

Congratulations. You have just solved mountain biking's most common problem!

Cautions for Safe Riding

As you develop your mountain biking skills, you will also develop more confidence in your abilities. But don't become overconfident. Just when you feel you can handle every situation, a new one arises. Always ride

WHEN YOUR CHAIN COMES OFF

Chain derailment is a problem most mountain bikers will have to face: Due to a quick or powerful shift, a bump, or a pedal hesitation, the bike chain jumps off the chainrings. The problem usually occurs on the large front chainrings but can occur on the rear freewheel. In either case, stop your bike immediately. Make sure you have shifted to the smallest chainring, and then gently pull part of the chain back onto the ring. Lift the rear wheel slightly, and turn the pedals slowly by hand until the chain slips completely back into position.

If the chain jumps inside the bigger ring in the rear, there is a greater chance of a jam (and of spoke damage). Gently pull and massage the chain to remove it if it has become wedged between the freewheel and the spokes.

safely, alertly, and within your comfort zone. Above all, never leave your helmet and other safety equipment at home.

Ride with a companion whenever possible; if you're riding alone always make sure someone knows where you're going and what time you expect to return.

There are untold factors that can cause a cycling accident and, unfortunately, the rider cannot control or predict every possibility. By being vigilant, prepared, and properly equipped, the rider can greatly reduce the chance for accident or injury.

Remember, good judgment is your most important tool.

SAFETY TIP It's a good idea to carry some money and personal identification on your person or in your seat pack. Paper money can be used for an emergency inside-the-tire patch and, of course, a little cash never hurts when thirst or hunger sets in. Carrying an ID is important in case an accident should occur. As an alternative, write your name, address, and phone number on the inside of your helmet.

PRERIDE SAFETY CHECKS

Smart cyclists check their bikes as well as their personal safety gear before each ride.

Feel your tires for air pressure. Check the quick releases on your front and rear wheels (this is especially important for riders who remove wheels regularly to transport the bike). Be sure your brakes are working. A common error is to take off a wheel and forget to reattach the brake cable and yoke after putting the wheel back on. Always check your brakes before pedaling off. Take a look to see that your brake pads are securely hitting the rims on each side. Spin the front and rear wheels and apply the brakes. Make sure the pads are making proper contact when braking.

Make sure your helmet is buckled securely around your chin. Wear protective glasses and gloves.

established companies that entered the business by offering road bike tours are now specializing in off-road, fat-tire tours and are finding new markets for their services.

Mountain biking has become a popular summertime activity at ski resort communities in the U.S. and abroad. Instead of closing down in the summer, ski lifts are carrying mountain bikers to mountain tops. Shedding their winter coats, ski runs become bike trails. Resort operators see mountain biking as a natural extension of their business: an environmentally conscious way to generate needed revenues at a time of year when their lodges and lifts were once quiet. Some resorts have opened complete mountain bike centers with instructional programs, rentals, marked trails, obstacle courses, mountain bike polo, and other organized activities.

Many ski resorts become mountain biking meccas during the summer months.

Wherever your riding takes you, remember to respect nature and don't trespass on private property. Make sure mountain bikes are allowed on the trail you want to ride. Mountain biking is allowed on most public land in the United States and open trail access is available in many other countries, but there are some restrictions and closed trails. For example, off-road riding is prohibited in U.S. national parks, although this policy can and should change, subject to certain limitations.

Finding the Best Local Rides

You'll quickly discover local roads and trails best suited to your riding tastes. To find new options, you might check with parks and forestry offices. More of these governmental units are developing trails and publishing trail maps.

Public parks can be well suited for novice and family riders. Trails are frequently gentle and well marked, trail maps are often available, and there are usually other riders in the area, an advantage if an emergency should occur.

Topographical (topo) maps that provide detailed elevation and distance information about specific areas are available in bike shops, camping and outdoor outlets, and from local printing and map or blueprint stores. (In the United States, the U.S. Geological Service produces excellent topo maps.) Local bike shops will often have wall maps or flyers describing favorite local rides.

Residents of smaller towns often find nice riding on dirt roads that wind into the surrounding countryside. Urban cyclists may have to travel a little farther before pedaling peacefully into the hills.

A peaceful country ride can provide a refreshing change of scenery for city dwellers.

If you have a shortage of trails in or near your community, be patient; they're coming. Local cities, counties, recreation commissions, bike clubs, and trails councils have recognized the need for more nonmotorized trails and many civic efforts are underway in this direction. Better yet, pitch in and help. Scout out trail locations, volunteer, and help make mountain biking more accessible in your area.

Day Trips and Weekends

After you've mastered the local trail loops, you'll be looking for new challenges. Check out trail or topographical maps of your nearest mountain recreation areas. Plan a day or weekend trip to an area that offers a pleasant and challenging ride, or sign up for a club ride.

Contact the local bike shops for firsthand trail information. Chambers of commerce, resort associations, and parks departments also can be of help. Getting the inside scoop from the locals always makes for a better ride. Don't be afraid to ask how steep or technical the trails are. Your ride should match your skill and fitness levels.

In some of the more popular mountain biking areas in California, Colorado, and other U.S. states, there has been a proliferation in recent years of local bike trail guides. These handy and informative booklets contain a wealth of local trail details and are usually well worth the investment of a few dollars per copy. There's no trail guide for your region? Write one.

Transporting Your Bike

Most mountain bikers transport their bikes in or on their personal vehicles. For greater distances, airplane and train bicycle transport is becoming more accepted.

Today's modern mountain bikes are easily disassembled, so many riders carry their bikes inside their vehicles. In many cases, all you have to do is remove a quick release front wheel and put your bike in the trunk or behind the seat in a station wagon or sport utility vehicle. With smaller vehicles, you may also have to remove the rear wheel. Advantages of carrying your bike inside include less chance of theft and less weather exposure.

Roof racks are popular these days. The roof rack has virtually been reinvented in recent years by companies such as Thule and Yakima. These new multipurpose racks have attachments for bikes as well as boards, kayaks, canoes, and skis. Expect to pay about $300 to $400 for a high-quality roof rack with bike attachments and locks. Fully loaded roof racks can carry up to six bikes, but four is a more comfortable number. Never drive into your garage with your roof rack loaded! This can cause serious damage to bike, vehicle, and home. And always make sure your rack and bikes are securely attached. You don't want to lose your load as you travel.

Roof racks help you get your bike to new places to ride.

Rear racks mount on the rear or trunk deck of your vehicle. They are small and convenient and most are easy to put on and take off. Most have a two- or three-bike carrying capacity. One drawback with most rear-mount racks is that they prevent access to trunk or rear-end doors or windows. A proper fit is imperative. Rear-mount racks can shift and vibrate, causing scuffing and scratching to your vehicle's paint. Always look for well-made, padded feet on a rear rack. Expect to pay $40 to $50 for low-end rear-mount racks and up to $100 or $120 for the best models.

If you drive a pickup, special bed racks allow you to secure your bikes so they don't bounce around.

Air transport can be expensive, but with more people taking cycling vacations and more businesspeople packing their bikes, air travel with bikes is becoming accepted. Normally you will pay a $40 to $60 excess baggage charge for your bike. Bike-friendly airlines will throw in a bike box for the price.

Bike shops are often prepared to pack your bike in a transport box for $20 or $25. Find a shop that offers this service, especially if you have an expensive bike. See how the bike is packed and next time try it yourself.

For packing, you must loosen the stem and turn or remove the handlebar. The front wheel and the pedals must also be removed.

Boxes work well, but if you and your bike are frequent travel companions, consider purchasing a soft- or hard-shell bike transport bag. They are expensive, $300 and up, but worth the investment in convenience and bicycle protection.

In most cases, train transport is easy and convenient. Your bike will be stowed in a baggage car without charge or special packaging.

AT A GLANCE: BIKE CARRIERS

Roof Racks

Advantages: Carries more. Frees trunk. Can carry other equipment.

Disadvantages: Expensive. Hard to reach and load. Driver must be on the lookout for overhead obstacles.

Rear Racks

Advantages: Inexpensive. Mounting rack is easy. Mounting bikes is easy. Collapsible.

Disadvantages: Prevents access to trunk. Carries only two or three bikes. Bikes and vehicles are more easily scratched and damaged.

Planning a Ride

As you look over maps and other literature to select a ride, try to look for new challenges but don't pick a ride that's too radical. Your route should be at least 90 percent ridable—a little uphill walking and pushing is all right to get to an exciting descent, but too much walking becomes tiresome.

When you're starting out, try to find off-road rides in the 5- to 15-mile (8- to 24-km) range. Keep in mind that it may take an hour or more to go 5 or 6 miles (8 or 10 km) in rugged terrain. Real trail conditions can be quite different from the way they appear on a map. For example, highly trained mountain bike racers who compete in extremely rugged conditions often average only 11 to 12 mph (18 to 19 kph). Plan plenty of time and don't be caught in unfamiliar areas after the sun goes down.

Ride with another person whenever possible because accidents are always a possibility, especially when you're exploring new turf. Be particularly careful when you're on a trail for the first time. The unexpected hazards can be many. If you do ride alone, make it a habit to tell someone what route you are following and when you will return.

Read your maps closely, and check elevation changes and total distance. When venturing more than walking distance from civilization, always plan your provisions; carry extra fluids, energy bars, and rain gear. A compass comes in handy on these rides and your cycle computer becomes more valuable.

Like the trappers, scouts, and explorers of frontier days, attune yourself with nature and your surroundings. Learn to follow tracks. That fat-tire track on the trail could lead to a very special ride.

Also remember that mountain bike riders must be especially careful not to trespass on private property. It's important for us to observe property rights and obey the law so that we don't create problems for other mountain bikers and the public image of mountain biking.

Riding the Ski Resorts

Ski areas have quickly and naturally become some of the most popular mountain bike gathering places. In the United States alone, close to 100 ski resorts transform themselves into mountain bike parks in what once was their off-season. At first the resorts were the domain of radical mountain bike kamikazes careening wildly down the slopes, but today they cater strongly to novices and families.

Prepare to pay $10 to $20 a day to ride up ski lifts with your bike and cruise down the resorts' trails. Some areas do not operate their lifts in the summer but still allow trail riding, usually with purchase of a trail pass. Cross-country ski areas often open their trails to mountain biking during the warm months. They also require a trail pass in most cases.

Nearly every resort with a mountain biking program offers bike and helmet rentals, so don't worry if a member of your group is short on equipment. Resort rentals are usually solid, durable, and well maintained.

Be sure to stay on marked trails. Many of the resorts have trail maps that show degree of trail difficulty. Often the resort's ski trail map will suffice. Recognize the standard trail marker signs: green for easiest, blue for more difficult, and black for most difficult. You probably won't want to bicycle down a double black diamond ski run!

Many resorts offer package mountain bike weekends or vacations, with a range of accommodations and dining choices. Or you may choose to stay at a nearby campground or bed and breakfast inn.

Remember, mountain weather is changeable so when heading to ski country, pack accordingly. Many resorts are at higher elevations so be sure to acclimatize yourself to avoid high altitude fatigue. Protect yourself against sunburn.

Mountain Bike Vacations

When you're ready to make tracks to the world's best mountain biking, you can do it on your own or use the services of a mountain bike tour operator.

By joining a tour, all the details are taken care of, leaving you to enjoy the ride. Support vehicles carry your gear, and meals and activities are provided at inns or camps along the trail. Experienced guides explain the geology, history, and culture of the area and offer tips to improve your riding techniques.

On the other hand, when traveling on your own, with family or friends, your schedule can be looser, you can set your own itinerary and pace, and you can change your plans on a whim. Stay where you wish by night and ride by day.

Biking vacations make for fun family getaways.

Cost, of course, may be your first consideration on how to travel. Is a tour experience worth the price or should you go it alone? A 5-day tour with premium accommodations and three meals a day may cost $850 to $1,100, or about $170 to more than $200 per day. A 5-day tour with campground accommodations will cost less, perhaps $600 to $700 for a 5-day trip.

If you will be riding for several days or a week, in addition to your camp gear and provisions, take an extra tire, a few tubes, a patch kit, an extra gear and brake cable, and basic tools, including crescent and Allen wrenches.

If you're traveling long distances for your tour, you may wish to rent a mountain bike instead of bringing your own. Rental of a high-quality bike adds about $100 to $120 to the 5-day tour price but may eliminate transportation costs and headaches. To ensure more comfortable riding, some riders bring their own bike seat and mount it on the rental bike.

Riders who choose self-guided tours to premium areas can expect to pay in the range of $80 to $100 per day for food and lodging. Remember, if you're touring on your own, you may need to purchase panniers and other gear, and this will add to the cost of your mountain bike vacation.

If you're visiting a premium destination, do you want to enjoy the area to its fullest? Maybe you should join a group for your first visit and return another time to explore the area with family or friends.

Most tours are geared toward the reasonably fit person, perhaps too slow for the highly tuned cyclist or too tough for the practiced couch potato. Good tours will match abilities or split groups and then rendezvous later in the day. Be prepared and in shape for a bike tour. You won't have an enjoyable ride if you can't keep up.

United States Getaways

Some of mountain biking's most notable destinations have emerged from early mountain bike festivals. First the racers came. Recreational riders, families, and tour companies weren't far behind.

In the United States, Crested Butte and Durango, Colorado; Moab, Utah; Mammoth Mountain and Big Bear Lake, California; Chequamegon, Wisconsin; Jim Thorpe, Pennsylvania; and Slaty Fork, West Virginia are popular and have gained widespread publicity through annual festivals. For a real glimpse into the world of mountain biking, a visit to one of these festivals should be on your vacation calendar.

Although it is a fast-growing sport and lifestyle, mountain biking has yet to have a significant effect on travel and leisure publishing. However, travel articles on mountain biking are beginning to appear more regularly and more attention is expected as the activity grows and matures, embracing new generations of travelers.

Listed here are just a few of the more recognized mountain bike centers. As you travel around your region, state, nation, or the globe enjoying mountain biking, you will undoubtedly discover other locations that deserve mention in future editions.

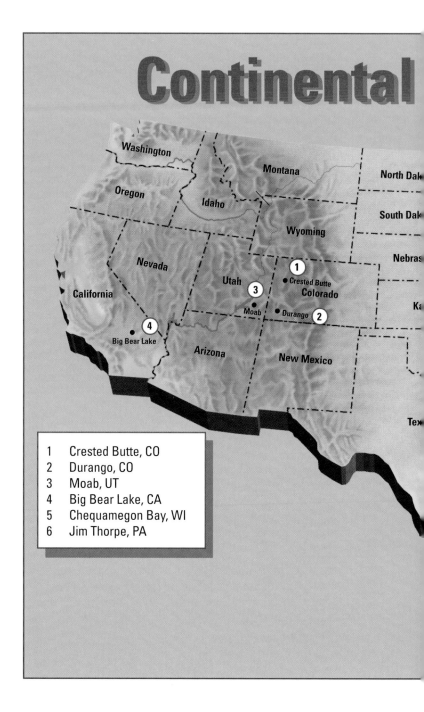

Continental

1 Crested Butte, CO
2 Durango, CO
3 Moab, UT
4 Big Bear Lake, CA
5 Chequamegon Bay, WI
6 Jim Thorpe, PA

nited States

5

nnesota · Chequamegon Bay

Wisconsin

Michigan

Iowa

Illinois Indiana Ohio

Missouri

Kentucky

Arkansas Tennessee

Louisiana

Mississippi

Alabama

Georgia

West Virginia Virginia

North Carolina

South Carolina

Florida

Maine

VT

NH

New York Mass.

Conn. RI

Pennsylvania

Jim Thorpe

6 NJ

MD Delaware

N

A YEAR-ROUND ACTIVITY

Cycling is no longer just a warm-weather sport. Modern equipment and all-weather apparel allow mountain bikers to ride comfortably year-round, and each season of the year has its own special rewards.

Die-hard riders can be seen pedaling around snow-covered mountain resort areas in midwinter, with studded tires on their bicycles. Some resorts have even held downhill mountain bike races on snowy courses.

David Epperson

My favorite riding season is autumn. The changing tones of the landscape, the cooler temperatures, and the end of season solitude make this a special time of year.

Dried leaves crunch and fly as you speed down a tree-lined lane. A leaf catches in your front brake, causing the whirring sound you used to get with playing cards and clothespins. A falling leaf brushes your cheek as you ride through the forest on a breezy fall day.

—Dave Carter

A MOUNTAIN BIKE VACATION GUIDE

An excellent mountain bike vacation guide is America's Greatest Trails Guide, a special collector's edition published in summer 1992 by *Mountain Bike Action* magazine (see appendix). The guide features the best American destinations and trails, including a state-by-state directory of U.S. ski resort riding, as well as ideas for rides in Europe, Australia, and New Zealand.

For a copy, contact *Mountain Bike Action,* Hi-Torque Publications, 10600 Sepulveda Blvd., Mission Hills, CA 91345.

MOAB, UTAH

Located in eastern Utah, Moab is famous in mountain bike circles for its slickrock terrain and it attracts curious riders from around the world. Cyclists enjoy scenic and technical riding on smooth red rock amid an outstanding desert backdrop. Moab's trails are reported to be among the most challenging anywhere. Moab hosts its annual Fat Tire Festival each October, the week before Halloween. Canyonlands and Arches national parks are nearby, as is the trailhead for the famous 100-mile (161-km) Kokopelli's Trail, a mountain bike route that follows ancient Indian trails. The area's best riding is in the spring and fall; summer can be too hot.

Sports File/Todd Powell

Slickrock Trail challenges bikers from all over the world.

CRESTED BUTTE, COLORADO

This old-fashioned Victorian ski town in the western part of the state is where Colorado mountain biking began. It is also home to the Mountain Bike Hall of Fame and Museum, a small but growing tribute to the sport. In early July each year, Crested Butte fills up with mountain bike enthusiasts for its annual Fat Tire Bike Week. Old mining roads and single-track trails lead from the town into the magnificent surrounding mountains. Challenging climbs and descents abound and numerous loops can be explored.

David Epperson

Taking a break at Crested Butte en route to Pefri Pass.

MAMMOTH MOUNTAIN, CALIFORNIA

Situated in the Sierra Nevada about 7 hours north of Los Angeles and 5 hours east of San Francisco, Mammoth is a world-renowned ski resort. In summer, it becomes one of mountain biking's premier destinations and it hosts a large mountain bike festival each year. A variety of riding is available on the ski mountain and throughout surrounding areas, including June Lake, Mono Lake, Convict Lake, and Devil's Postpile. Mammoth became one of the first major resorts to embrace mountain biking. It hosted the NORBA World Mountain Bike Championships from 1987 to 1989 (coauthor Don Davis won the veteran class—age 35-plus—cross-country world championship in 1987 and placed second in 1988).

OTHER U.S. DESTINATIONS

Fine mountain bike destinations across the U.S. are receiving attention through festivals, races, and instructional programs. Excellent trail systems are being expanded and made more accessible to all levels of cyclists.

In the east, Mt. Snow, Vermont, has led the ski resort movement into mountain biking. It has operated a mountain bike school for several years and offers a wide variety of easy to very technical roads and trails. In New Hampshire's White Mountains and all across New England, today's more active leaf-lookers are taking autumn foliage tours on a range of scenic mountain bike trails.

Some of New England's most scenic routes can be found in Maine's Acadia National Park.

Lake Minnewaska State Park in New York's Hudson River country features more than 100 miles (161 km) of shale-packed roads and trails that beckon mountain bikers. Located near the town of New Paltz, the area offers fine scenery around Lake Armstrong and great views across the Catskill Mountains.

This is a good destination for both beginning and experienced riders who want to enjoy a weekend adventure. It is a convenient getaway for riders from the bustling New York metropolis.

Nearby Allaire State Park near Longbranch, New Jersey, and Ringwood State Park near Paramus, New Jersey, offer single-track and fire road rides. Steep Rock Reserve near Washington Depot, Connecticut, is a picturesque area with an abundance of beginner and intermediate terrain.

Other growing mountain bike centers in the eastern and central parts of the United States include Jim Thorpe, Pennsylvania, a small town in the Pocono Mountains that hosts its annual Mountain Bike Weekend Off-Road Festival every June; Chequamegon, in upstate Wisconsin, host of the Midwest's largest off-road festival and the Chequamegon 40 off-road race, held each summer; and Slaty Fork, West Virginia, home of the West Virginia Fat Tire Festival, held each year in mid-June.

Durango, Colorado, is a true mountain bike town and home to several of mountain biking's top competitors. It has hosted national competitions, and it holds a mountain bike festival every July and the annual Iron Horse Bicycle Classic festival (off- and on-road biking) every Memorial Day weekend. Vail is another Rocky Mountain destination. It offers mountain bike access to untamed high country scenery through the famed 10th Mountain Division trail and hut system. Sun Valley and Ketchum, Idaho, are base areas for rides to the lakes, old mines, and hot springs in the Sawtooth National Recreation Area.

Marin County, California, the birthplace of mountain biking, has trails winding through Mt. Tamalpais and Pine Mountain and beyond to Point Reyes National Seashore, although many of Mt. Tam's trails have been closed because of conflicts with hikers and other users. The Bodega Bay area to the north also offers scenic seaside riding. There is fine riding throughout the Sierra Nevada mountains, including in the Lake Tahoe area. In Southern California, the Snow Summit resort at Big Bear Lake holds summer and fall mountain bike festivals, attracting riders from the Los Angeles metropolitan area 2 hours away.

Western Europe by Mountain Bike

Mountain biking is a made-in-America sport that has been warmly embraced in Europe. American racer Mike Kloser won the 1988 World Mountain Bike Championships at Crans Montana, Switzerland, and the 1988 World Cup Finals at Torbole, Italy. Kloser, a resident of Vail, Colorado, lived, trained, and raced in Europe for 2 years.

"In many of the European areas, you'll find an abundance of more difficult terrain," says Kloser. "You'll encounter private trails and lanes but most of the time you will be allowed to pass through. There are many pedestrian paths and trails that were not designed for mountain bikes but

European Destinations

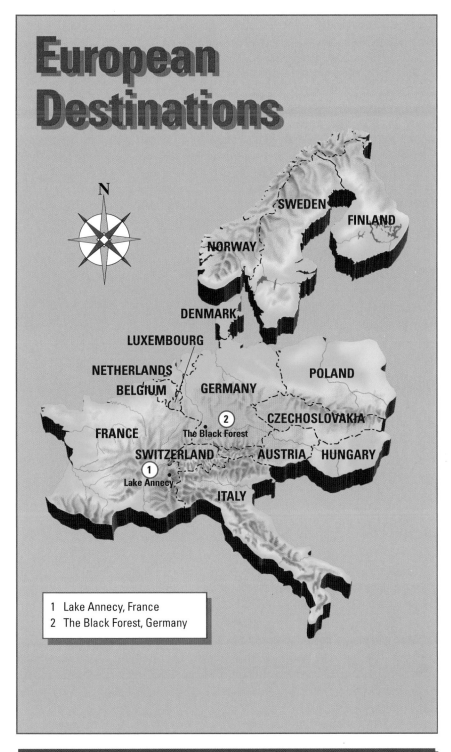

1 Lake Annecy, France
2 The Black Forest, Germany

if you demonstrate a polite attitude and cautious approach, you'll find there won't be too much conflict.''

Kloser lists these favorites:

ANZERE, SWITZERLAND

This area, located above the Valley of Sion and across from Crans Montana, offers an abundance of good trails and unpaved roads. Views of the snow-covered Matterhorn and Mt. Blanc can be seen from the hillside trails. There is a good mountain bike visitor program that offers guided rides, maps, and well-marked trails.

BIENNE, SWITZERLAND

Located near the northwest corner of Switzerland, this area is home to 1992 women's world champion, Sylvia Furst. The trails are diverse; many of the best rides are connected by sections of pavement. Great views overlook the lakes surrounding Bienne.

Switzerland is one big mountain biking opportunity.

LAKE ANNECY, FRANCE

Located about an hour west of Geneva and a half-hour north of the Olympic village of Albertville, this is a picturesque area in the foothills of the Alps. The hillsides around the lake are loaded with fun trails of all kinds, ranging from four-wheel-drive tracks to wooded and twisting single-tracks. The town offers a taste of the French lifestyle, and the lake has a variety of water sports.

David Epperson

The French Alps.

LAGO DIGARDA, ITALY

This is a summer tourist area situated in north-central Italy, just south of the Alps and Dolomites. Numerous trails circle the lake, with many heading off into the surrounding hills. Some use parts of old Roman roadways made of cobblestone. Plenty of local vineyards are found in the area.

THE BLACK FOREST, GERMANY

The Black Forest, near Baden Baden, is a favorite riding and training area for German cyclists. The wooded, rolling hills have many trails and old logging roads. Visitors should stop at the old Roman baths in the historic town of Baden Baden (which translates to bath bath).

MORE EUROPEAN FAVORITES

Other riders have reported fine riding opportunities throughout the mountainous regions of France, Spain, Germany, Austria, and Switzerland. Some of the world's most scenic mountain terrain is found in the Alpine countries of Europe.

Good riding has been reported in the Pyrenees along the Spanish–French border, in the small towns of the Bavarian Alps, such as Garmisch and Berchtesgaden, and in many resort communities in the Austrian Alps. Good reports have come from riders visiting the Bernese Oberland of Switzerland including Interlaken, Grindelwald, Wengen, and Murren. The famed peaks Eiger and Jungfrau are in this region. The Davos-Klosters area has hosted World Cup racing.

David Epperson

Biking in Tuscany, Italy, affords glimpses of picturesque villas.

Franklin Henry, a Colorado-based pro racer who has ridden in many countries, suggests riding in the southern reaches of the Black Forest, near Freiburg, Germany, where long asphalt bike trails lead to a wide network of off-road trails, including flat and mountainous terrain. Scenery includes farms, trains, castle ruins, and old battlefields. Local bike shops have maps that show trails as well as historical attractions.

Henry also likes the Strasbourg area just north in the Rhine River valley, which features excellent riding through rolling valleys and vineyards. He also suggests the hills above Munich, where nice terrain and guided tours are available.

In southeastern Belgium, Henry recommends the Ardennes area, which includes Hoffalize, a World Cup race site. The area features hilly to mountainous terrain with rich forests and abundant single-track trails.

Bike Britain

Well-known British cyclist Simon Burney, author of a book on mountain bike racing and manager of a mountain bike race team, is enthusiastic about the riding opportunities in Great Britain. He recommends national parks in the mountainous areas, where the trails are challenging and the scenery is attractive.

Burney cautions that off-road riding is allowed only on public bridleways and that in some sensitive areas, even the bridleways are closed. The British Mountain Bike Federation has developed links with other outdoor groups and is working to expand mountain bike access.

"Don't be put off by the wet weather attributed to the British Isles," Burney says. "The island climate means constant changes. Wet weather seldom stays long. A rainy day can turn sunny in a few hours."

First National Park in the Peak District of Derbyshire is located at the south end of the Pennine Chain (the Backbone of Britain). Popular with tourists, and a training ground for most British professional cyclists, it features a variety of riding terrain at Moorlands and Rocky Edges.

The Lake District is one of Britain's most popular mountain areas. England's highest mountains are found here, topped by Scafell Pikes. Stunning scenery and lakes abound.

Scotland offers Britain's highest mountains, including Ben Nevis. The Aviemore ski area is popular among mountain bikers, having hosted World Cup races 1988 through 1991.

Stockfile/Steven Behr

The white cliffs of Dover offer a scenic ride in southern England.

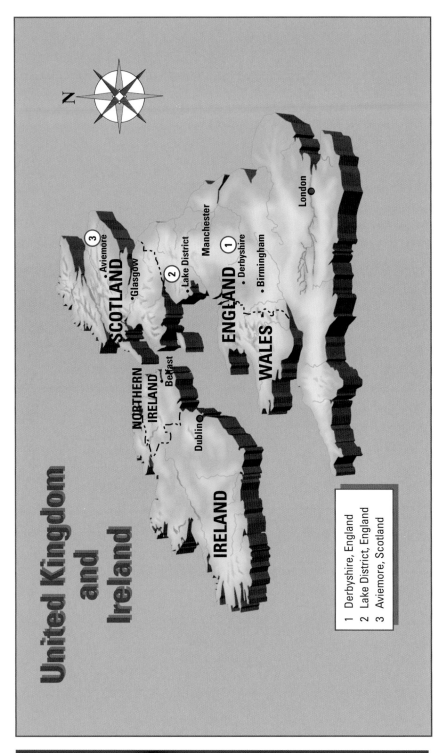

United Kingdom and Ireland

N

IRELAND

NORTHERN IRELAND

Dublin

Belfast

SCOTLAND

Aviemore ③

Glasgow

Lake District ②

Manchester

ENGLAND

Derbyshire ①

Birmingham

WALES

London

1 Derbyshire, England
2 Lake District, England
3 Aviemore, Scotland

Canada's Trails

In Canada, mountain bikers have discovered fine trails in the Whistler-Blackcomb resort areas of British Columbia. Franklin Henry is partial to the town of Squamish just north of Vancouver and its beautiful trails along the Strait of Georgia.

Mountain bikers also are taking in the grandeur of the Canadian Rockies resort areas near Banff. To the east, the Bromont resort in Quebec has hosted world-class competitions.

THE WEST

Highlands in Victoria, British Columbia, features an extensive maze of fire roads and trails for exploration by all levels of mountain bikers. Another favorite, near Lake Mathison Park, is the Galloping Goose Trail, a scenic route that follows 80 kilometers (50 miles) of old railroad trail.

On the highway between Banff and Jasper in Alberta.

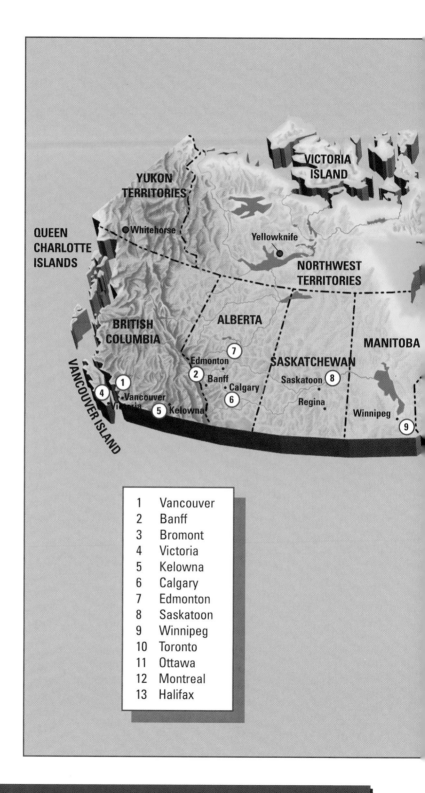

1	Vancouver
2	Banff
3	Bromont
4	Victoria
5	Kelowna
6	Calgary
7	Edmonton
8	Saskatoon
9	Winnipeg
10	Toronto
11	Ottawa
12	Montreal
13	Halifax

riding throug[...]
Ontario, offe[...]
mountain bik[...]

Parc De P[...]
mountain bik[...]
trails, cross-[...]
most challer[...]
also offers f[...]

THE ATLAN[...]
Jimmy's R[...]
rocky singl[...]
local favor[...]

Scenic A[...]
and New[...]

Mountair[...]
bike tour[...]
the endle[...]
can take[...]
tainous[...]

Austr[...]
Sydney[...]
hosted[...]

Fine[...]
known[...]
Park, v[...]

In N[...]
compe[...]
and th[...]

Sw[...]
is stil[...]
gover[...]
priva[...]

Th[...]
acro[...]
sugg[...]
hot[...]
hub[...]
Tau[...]

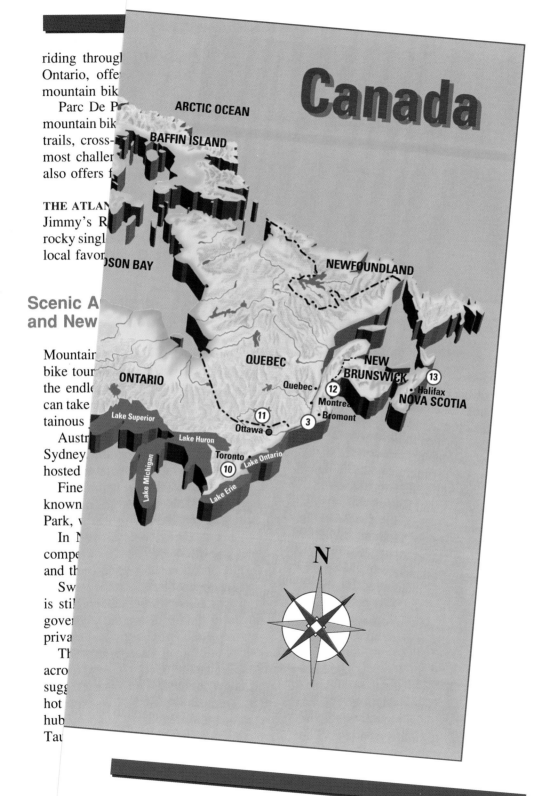

The Vanc

The
terrain
difficu
offer c
Ket
terrain
rated
BC, i
Th
Albe
Cree
and
In
cros
F
of s
for

TH
Se
su
cr
a

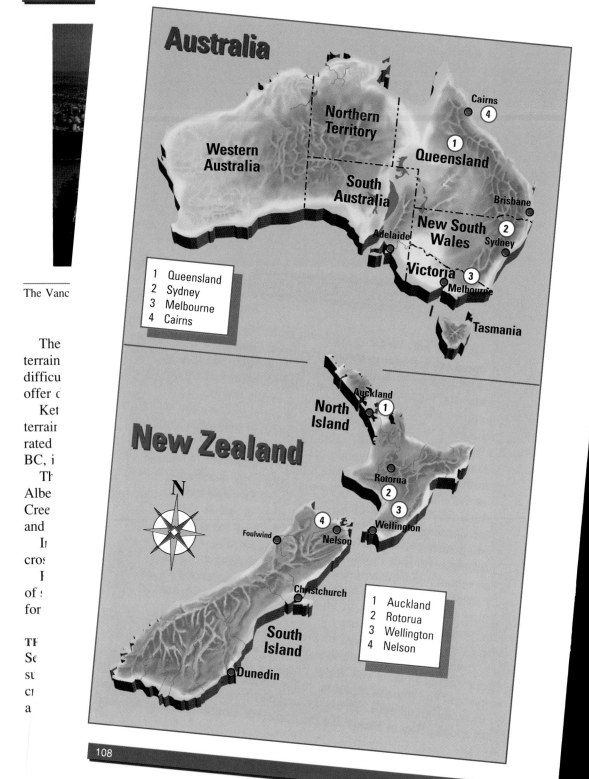

Lake Rotoetti in New Zealand—a scene of peaceful reflection.

offers spectacular riding around three volcanos. The Wellington area, at the southern end of North Island, offers riding on roads and trails in the hills surrounding coastal resorts.

Nelson, at the north end of South Island, is at the base of a mountainous area, and many of its trails climb into the higher elevations. Lake Tekapo borders the Southern Alps in the central part of South Island and offers many possibilities for exploring around small lakes. Finally, Swart suggests the area north of Marlborough Sound, on South Island, for riding through forests overlooking scenic bays.

first-timers as well as for age and skill level. In the U.S., most races sanctioned by the National Off-Road Bicycle Association (NORBA) will issue one-day race licenses to beginning racers. Many riders enter races just for fun and to measure their own abilities by charting their development as riders. Race against yourself, not against the pack.

Competition categories in most mountain bike races include Beginner, for the first-time competitor; Sport, for the intermediate competitor; Expert, for the advanced competitor; and Pro/Elite, status granted on request.

Age classes are Junior, ages 12-18; Senior, ages 19-34; Veteran, ages 35-44; and Master, age 45 and older.

Just another day at the races.

TYPES OF RACES

There are several different types of mountain bike competitions, ranging from endurance events such as cross-country races to exciting, fast-paced action such as the downhill. If any of these events seems exciting to you, pursue it!

Cross-country—A mass start event contested on dirt roads and trails, and sometimes on a limited amount of pavement. Cross-country races are usually held on circuits of 2 miles (3.2 km) or longer.

Point-to-point—A mass start event starting at one point and ending at another. Terrain is similar to a cross-country race.

Hill climb—A timed event with either individual or mass starts. As the name indicates, the course climbs to a finish at a higher elevation than the start. Hill climbs can range from moderate to some of the toughest endurance tests in the world.

Downhill—An exciting event for riders and spectators, the downhill is the most dangerous of mountain bike races. It is usually an individual time trial with starts at specific intervals, such as 30 seconds or 1 minute. Each racer is timed from the start to a lower elevation finish line.

Dual slalom—Riders compete next to one another on side-by-side courses in a format similar to dual slalom ski racing. The rider must go through each gate on his or her own course. Riders switch courses for a second run. The best combined time from two runs wins. Penalties are assessed for false starts, crashing, or missing a gate.

Stage race—A stage race might typically include a cross-country, up-hill, and downhill. Winners of each event are recognized with points, and the rider with the total point lead or lowest combined time is the overall winner. This event is a good measurement of all-around skills.

Ultraendurance—Mountain biking's answer to the marathon. Ultra-endurance races are more than 75 miles (121 km) long.

Observed Trials

Trials competitions are one of mountain biking's most interesting spectator events. Held in a compact, arena-like setting, trials events often attract large crowds. In trials, riders must negotiate a series of challenging obstacle courses. Obstacles may include logs, large rocks, giant boulders, water, mud, a combination of these, and severely uneven terrain.

Most trials events have stock and modified bicycle classes. Riders compete on regular mountain bikes in the stock class; serious trials riders compete in the modified bike class using small, specially designed trials bikes with 20-inch wheels.

Just one of many obstacles in the trials at Mt. Snow, Vermont.

The trials competitor attempts to ride over or through each obstacle, staying within set boundaries and not putting a foot on the ground. Putting a foot down is called a dab. When a rider completes a section without dabbing or going out of bounds he is said to have ''cleaned'' the section.

Trials are scored on points, with the lowest total winning. Each dab is a point against you. Five points is the worst you can score in one section.

Most trials events have 5 to 10 sections in which the rider is judged and scored. There are individual and combined winners.

Stunts

Mountain bike stunts are best learned from more experienced riders. Go to a trials event and you will see stunts you would never have imagined. Talk to the competitors; most will be happy to give you a few pointers on how to practice.

Many advanced trials maneuvers are more difficult than they may appear when performed by an expert rider so be careful in your attempts.

For example, if you want to learn to jump obstacles, start with small, forgiving objects. Jump over a styrofoam cup and practice until you are

Difficult stunts like this require expert skill.

perfect every time before you try progressively higher jumps like a curb, log, or park bench.

These stunts can take as much or more time to master than training for a cross-country mountain bike race. Stunts can be fun but be prepared to take some tumbles if this is your kind of thrill.

Mountain Bike Polo

This is a hot social sport that is gaining popularity with mountain bikers around the globe. The only specialized equipment needed are mallets and balls which may be obtained through the World Bicycle Polo Federation (see the appendix) or a dealer near you.

Mountain bike polo is played on a flat field, 160 feet (48.8 m) long by 90 feet (27.4 m) wide, with 12-foot (3.7-m) wide goals at each end. A match consists of two 10-minute time periods called chukkers.

"It's not an endurance sport. It's more strategy than stamina," says Zachi Anderson, owner of a bicycle shop in Grass Valley, California, and a member of the 1989 California state champion bicycle polo team.

The official rule book calls for four-person coed teams. The ball may be played only parallel to the sidelines to avoid dangerous collisions. Anderson says a typical strategy is a rotating play where riders ride through the goal zone and then circle back down the sideline and back onto the field of play.

According to Anderson, a typical match might include 10 or 12 goals, although good defensive teams can often hold the opposition scoreless.

John Laptad/F-Stock

A new way to compete on a bike—playing polo.

Moab, Utah, hosts a World Bicycle Polo Championship each October as part of its annual Fat Tire Festival. The event has attracted teams from across the United States.

Training

Consistency is the key to successful training for any mountain bike competition. Work on increasing your workouts in both length and intensity. Develop and follow a cycling program and consider cross-training. This will improve your cycling and help avoid burnout from overtraining. Weight lifting will increase your strength, and running will help you aerobically. Cross-country and downhill skiing, ice skating, and in-line skating work many of the same muscles as cycling and are cross-training methods used by competitive mountain bikers.

Make It Fun

Enter a competitive event with some of your cycling pals. Don't worry about winning; pace each other and measure your abilities against the best racers or trials competitors in the field. Enter the proper class as a beginner and you will improve rapidly. To be successful, you need to master the basics. Work on fitness and practice technique and maneuvers in a variety of terrains.

This kind of intense competition requires a consistent training regimen.

Mountain biking at advanced levels requires time and practice. Focus your efforts on climbing, descending, cornering, shifting, braking, and riding over obstacles smoothly and efficiently. As you ride, read the terrain. Braking, shifting, and balancing through the technical sections will become second nature. Your level of skill will develop in time. Be patient; learn to control your speed and if a section of trail is too difficult, get off and walk or carry your bike. Go back later and ride the tough, technical sections. Don't be too quick to judge yourself against the racers.

Riding with others is the key to riding faster and farther. The best way to develop greater proficiency is to take on new terrain with others who are at or slightly above your skill level. If your companion is a much better rider, you will suffer at his or her pace. Plus, your safety could be at stake.

If there is a mountain bike club or race group in your area, join in on a ride. You will quickly identify your strengths and weaknesses. Are you a strong climber? A downhill daredevil? Get together with some friends for some mountain bike polo, a true test of bike handling skills. Or test yourself at a trials event. Go to a race as a spectator and watch the pros tackle the toughest obstacle or course. Visualize yourself in their position.

SAFETY TIP Before a competition, or any ride for that matter, check your brakes, brake-pad–wheel alignment, tire pressure, cable tensions, and gears. Pay attention to your gear adjustments; a mountain bike event will almost always demand that your low range gears work perfectly.

Make sure your stem bolt and handlebars are tight; steering can be stressed during tough race conditions. Finally, check the quick releases on your wheels and make sure they are firmly in place, but not overtightened.

If you are not confident in making these adjustments on your own, check with your bike shop for advice.

SAMPLE RACE TRAINING PROGRAM

Here's a basic training program to use as a guideline:

Monday: 1 to 2 hours of steady pedaling on easy terrain at a cadence of 90 to 110 revolutions per minute. Easy spinning, no big gears. If you use a heart rate monitor or measure your pulse manually, use a target 10 or 20 beats below your maximum heart rate (remember, 220 minus your age equals maximum heart rate). For best results, most of your training should be in the 60 percent to 85 percent range of maximum.

Tuesday: 1 hour to 90 minutes of off-road riding with average heart rate in the 60 percent to 85 percent range.

Wednesday: 1 to 2 hours of riding at 70 percent to 85 percent of maximum. This should simulate race pace and duration.

Thursday: Intensity near maximum. Warm up for a half-hour, then begin intervals. These are 45- to 60-second bursts at near maximum effort. Progress to six or eight efforts, with adequate recovery time between. For maximum effect, intervals can be increased to 2 to 3 minutes each. Be sure your heart rate returns below the threshold level before doing the next interval. These intervals will simulate the first mile or so of a mountain bike race, allowing you to make this kind of effort and then recover for optimum performance throughout the race.

Friday: Rest.

Saturday: 1 hour to 90 minutes of easy riding at 60 percent of your maximum heart rate.

Sunday: Race day. Good luck!

If you are limited by time, which we all are, try to train for at least 40 to 60 minutes per day at or near your training threshold. It is generally agreed that 20 minutes at this level will generate a training effect.

Make your training fun and not too regimented. Alternate your easy and hard days. Remember, it is best to be well rested coming into a race.

Your overall fitness is best maintained with some activity every day (20 to 40 minutes) that will increase your heart rate. Fitness needs to be part of daily life, especially as we get older.

APPENDIX

FOR MORE INFORMATION

Cycling Organizations

Bicycle Federation of Australia, Inc.
P.O. Box 869
Artarmon, NSW 2064 Australia
(02) 412-1041

Bicycle Institute of America (BIA)
1818 R St., NW
Washington, DC 20009 USA
(202) 332-6986/fax (202) 332-6989

Bikecentennial
P.O. Box 8308
Missoula, MT 59807 USA
(406) 721-1776

British Mountain Bike Federation
36 Rockingham Rd.
Kettering, Northampton, England
(44) 536-412211/fax (44) 536-412142

Canadian Cycling Association (CCA)
1600 James Naismith
Gloucester, ON, Canada K1B 5N4

International Mountain Bicycling Association (IMBA)
P.O. Box 412043
Los Angeles, CA 90041 USA
(818) 792-8830/fax (818) 796-2299

League of American Wheelmen (LAW)
190 West Ostend St., Suite 120
Baltimore, MD 21230 USA
(410) 539-3399

Mountain Bike Hall of Fame and Museum
P.O. Box 845
Crested Butte, CO 81224 USA
(303) 349-7382

National Off-Road Bicycle Association (NORBA)
1750 East Boulder St.
Colorado Springs, CO 80909 USA
(719) 578-4717/fax (719) 578-4596

United States Bicycling Hall of Fame
34 East Main St.
Somerville, NJ 08876 USA
(800) BICYCLE or (201) 722-3620

United States Cycling Federation (USCF)
1750 East Boulder St.
Colorado Springs, CO 80909 USA
(719) 578-4581

Women's Mountain Biking and Tea Society (WOMBATS)
P.O. Box 757
Fairfax, CA 94930 USA

World Bicycle Polo Federation
P.O. Box 1039
Bailey, CO 80421 USA
(303) 838-7431

Science
Edmun
Human
Box 50
Champ
$15.95

Periodi

Austra
P.O. B
Artarm
(02) 4

Bicycle
545 B
Boston
(617)

Bicycle
33 E.
Emma
(215)

Bikere
Bikece
P.O. E
Misso
(406)

Cyclir
Unitec
1750
Color
(719)

Dirt R
AKA
460 N
Spring
(412)

Books

All-Terrain Biking: Skills and Techniques for Mountain Bikers
Jim Zarka
Bicycle Books
P.O. Box 2038
Mill Valley, CA 94941 USA
$7.95

Bicycle Mechanics
Steve Snowling and Ken Evans
Human Kinetics
Box 5076
Champaign, IL 61825-5076 USA
$18.95

Bicycle Technology
Rob van der Plas
Bicycle Books
P.O. Box 2038
Mill Valley, CA 94941 USA
$16.95

Cuthbertson's Little Mountain Bike Book
Tom Cuthbertson
Ten Speed Press
P.O. Box 7123
Berkeley, CA 94707 USA
$5.95

Mountain Bike! A Manual of Beginning to Advanced Technique
William Nealy
Menasha Ridge Press
3169 Cahaba Heights Rd.
Birmingham, AL 35243 USA
$12.95

Mountain Bike Handbook
Rob van der Plas
Sterling
387 Park Ave. S
New York, NY 10016 USA
$10.95

Mou
Rob
Bicy
P.O.
Mill
$14.

Mou
Tim
Spri
Nor
Hud
Wes
$22.

The
Der
Lyo
31 '
Nev
$12

Mo
Der
Lyc
31
Nev
$7.

Mo
Joh
Bic
P.C
Mi
$2.

Mc
Mi
IC
Or
10
Mc
$6

IMBA Trail News
International Mountain Bicycling Association
P.O. Box 1212
Crested Butte, CO 81224 USA
(303) 349-7104

Mountain and City Biking
7950 Deering Ave.
Canoga Park, CA 91304 USA
(818) 887-0550

Mountain Bike Action
Hi-Torque Publications
10600 Sepulveda Blvd.
Mission Hills, CA 91345 USA
(818) 365-6831

NORBA News
National Off-Road Bicycle Association
1750 E. Boulder St.
Colorado Springs, CO 80909 USA
(719) 578-4717/fax (719) 578-4596

Pedal
Canadian Cycling News
2 Pardee Ave., Suite 204
Toronto, ON, Canada M6K 3H5
(416) 530-1350/fax (416) 530-4155

Competition Periodicals

Velo News
1830 N. 55th St.
Boulder, CO 80301 USA
(303) 440-0601

Winning
744 Roble Rd., Suite 190
Allentown, PA 18103 USA
(215) 266-6893

Bicycle Trade Magazines

American Bicyclist
Cycling Press
80 Eighth Ave.
New York, NY 10011 USA
(212) 206-7230/fax (212) 633-0079

Bicycle Business Journal
P.O. Box 1570
Fort Worth, TX 76101 USA
(817) 870-0341/fax (817) 332-1619

Bicycle Retailer & Industry News
1444-C S. St. Francis Dr.
Santa Fe, NM 87501 USA
(505) 988-5099/fax (505) 988-7224

Bicycle Today
Bicycle Today Magazine Co.
5, Lane, 226, Sung Chiang Rd.
Taipei, Taiwan, ROC
(02) 5718626

Mail Order Catalogs

Bike Nashbar
4111 Simon Rd.
Youngstown, OH 44512-1343 USA
(216) 782-2244

California Bicycle Supply
P.O. Box 470502
San Francisco, CA 94123 USA
(415) 349-9539 or (800) 999-4745

Campmor
P.O. Box 998
Paramus, NJ 07653 USA
(201) 445-5000

The Colorado Cyclist
3970 E. Bijou St.
Colorado Springs, CO 80909-9946 USA
(719) 591-4040 or (800) 688-8600

Excel Sports International
3275 Prairie Ave., Suite 1
Boulder, CO 80301 USA
(303) 444-6737 or (800) 627-6664

LL Bean, Inc.
LL Street
Freeport, ME 04033 USA
(800) 221-4221

Performance Bicycle
P.O. Box 2741
Chapel Hill, NC 27515-2741 USA
(800) 727-2433

Tours and Travel

Backroads Bicycle Touring (worldwide)
1516 Fifth St.
Berkeley, CA 94710-1740 USA
(510) 527-1555
(800) 245-3874

Cycle America (U.S.)
P.O. Box 29B
Northfield, MN 55057 USA
(800) 245-3263

Outer Edge Expeditions (heli-lift mountain biking, New Zealand)
45500 Pontiac Trail
Walled Lake, MI 48390 USA
(313) 624-5140 or (800) 322-5235

Tailwinds Bicycle Tours (Australia)
72 Wattle St.
Lyneham, ACT 2602 Australia
(06) 249-6122

Timberline Bicycle Tours (Rocky Mountains, Pacific states)
7975 E. Harvard, #J
Denver, CO 80231 USA
(303) 759-3804

VCC Four Seasons Cycling (U.S. East Coast, eastern Canada)
P.O. Box 145
Waterbury Center, VT 05677 USA
(802) 244-5135

Western Spirit Cycling (Rocky Mountains)
P.O. Box 411
Moab, UT 84532 USA
(801) 259-8732 or (800) 845-BIKE

MOUNTAIN BIKING LINGO

access—Term used to describe riding areas available to mountain bikers, as in public land access.

aerobic exercise—Muscular activity that is fueled by oxygen.

anaerobic exercise—Muscular activity at an intense rate, not fueled by oxygen. Such exercise can be maintained for only a short time; oxygen is eventually required to enable recovery.

bonk—To run out of energy.

braze-on fitting—A piece soldered to the frame (usually with silver or brass) for attaching such extras as water bottle cages and cable guide eyelets.

bunny hop—A maneuver to jump obstacles such as logs, rocks, or curbs in which both wheels leave the ground. In a wheelie hop, only the front tire leaves the ground.

cantilever brakes—Style of brakes most common to the mountain bike and hybrid bike. Attached by two bosses that are brazed on the front and rear fork stays.

chain breaker—Tool for pushing pin in or out to attach or remove chain. Also called a chain tool.

cleaning a section—Riding over an area without putting a foot down.

clunker—An old-fashioned 26-inch single-speed bike, or the very earliest design of mountain bike.

crank—Arm that attaches the pedal to the bottom-bracket spindle.

cyclo-cross bike—Bike similar to a road bike, with turned-down handlebar, cantilever brakes, and narrow tires. Used for cyclo-cross training and racing on part-dirt, part-pavement courses.

derailleur—Mechanism in front and rear that moves the chain between gears.

downshift—To shift to a lower, or easier, gear.

endo—A dramatic over-the-handlebar crash. See *face-plant*.

etiquette—Showing good judgment in trail use and respecting other users.

face-plant—A nasty wreck in which the rider eats dirt. May or may not be an endo.

fall line—The most direct route down a hill.

fat tire—The kind of tire used on a mountain bike. Also a term used to describe mountain bike–related things, as in fat tire festival.

fire road—Single lane, one-vehicle-width roads in the hills that serve as fire breaks and allow emergency vehicle access.

gonzo—Crazy; somewhat weird.

granny gear—Small chainring, used mainly for climbing.

hub—Center of wheel; point at which spokes attach.

index shifting—Sometimes referred to as click shifting. Changing one gear up or down for each click stop in the particular derailleur system used.

kamikaze—A daredevil mountain biker.

panniers—Luggage carriers for touring.

quick release—Lever mechanism for easy removal and attachment of wheels or seat.

single-track—Narrow trail on which cyclists must ride in single file. A double-track trail allows two bikes side by side.

slickrock—Smooth rock hills that offer challenging riding (a Utah specialty).

stem—The piece that attaches the handlebar to the frame.

step-in pedal—Enables stable attachment between cleated shoe and pedal. A sideward twist will usually release the connection. Also known as clipless pedal.

suspension—Design feature that provides shock absorption. Front suspension can be through suspension forks or stem. Rear suspension can use a pivoting rear triangle or suspended seat lever. *Fully suspended* is a term used to describe a bike with front and rear suspension.

switchback—A 90-degree or greater turn on a road or trail.

toe clip—Pedal attachment that helps hold the foot on the pedal. Usually combined with a toe strap.

topo map—A localized topographical map showing elevations and other geographic features.

U-brake—Style of brake. Used as a rear brake on some bikes.

upshift—To shift into a higher, or harder, gear.

INDEX

ABOUT THE AUTHORS

Don Davis   **Dave Carter**

Don Davis is a sponsorship coordinator for Bell Sports, Inc. He is also an expert on mountain biking, having been involved in the activity since the late 1970s when it was just beginning to develop. In addition to recreational riding, Don has spent more than a decade racing mountain bikes on the professional and veteran mountain biking circuits. In 1987 he finished first in the Veteran Mountain Bike Cross Country World Championships, and in 1988 he finished second.

Before getting involved in mountain biking, Don competed both nationally and internationally in road bicycling for over 20 years. He was the 1968 California State Junior Road Champion.

Don received his bachelor's degree in health science from San Jose State University in 1973. He is a member of both the National Off-Road Bicycle Association and the United States Cycling Federation. Don now lives in Campbell, CA, where in his free time he enjoys skiing, tennis, swimming, and hiking.

Dave Carter is a freelance writer and a community relations specialist who resides in Nevada City, CA. As a longtime skier and former ski

patrolman, he took up mountain biking as a way to stay in shape for ski season. He became hooked and now rides year-round.

Dave has an extensive writing background including 12 years experience as a writer and correspondent for major daily newspapers. He also has had numerous articles published in leading travel, outdoor, and sports magazines. Whenever he gets the chance, Dave combines his job as a writer with his love for biking. He not only has worked as a publicist for the West Coast's first mountain bike park at the Eagle Mountain ski area, but also has helped promote and publicize the Tour of Nevada City Bicycle Classic.

Dave received his bachelor's degree in mass communications from California State University at Fullerton in 1973. His leisure activities include skiing, softball, and cycling.

Photo Credits

Pages 4, 5 (top), 6 (top): Special thanks to TREK USA
9, 26-27, 31, 47: Courtesy of Bell Sports
17: Rich Cruse/courtesy of Bell Sports
18: Malcolm Fearon/Singletrack Photography
32, 53, 54: Mark Thayer/courtesy of Bell Sports
22, 35, 67-69, 72-74: Wilmer Zehr/special thanks to Champaign Cycle Co.
37, 76, 112, 114, 117: Tom Moran/Singletrack Photography
56, 82: Beth Schneider
65, 88: Bob Winsett/TOM STACK & ASSOCIATES
83: Neal A. Palumbo/Singletrack Photography
98: Spencer Swanger/TOM STACK & ASSOCIATES
103, 109: Markham Johnson/Backroads Bicycle Touring
106: Paul Morrison, Box 162, Whistler, British Columbia, Canada V0N 1B0
115: Alan Hardy/courtesy of Bell Sports